Elusive Things

A Novel

From one insomniac
to another.

Steven B. Golub

PublishAmerica
Baltimore

ISBN: 1-60441-537-1
PUBLISHED BY PUBLISHAMERICA, LLLP
www.publishamerica.com
Baltimore

Printed in the United States of America

This book is dedicated to my two great kids, Scott and Jordana, my stepson, Joseph and to my beautiful wife, Catherine who is my very best friend and inspiration.

For my Dad, whose life cut short at 55, never saw what became of his adult son. And for my mom who misses him everyday.

It is also dedicated to my friend, Mike who is now fighting cancer for the third time in as many years.

PART I

Like as the waves make towards the pebbled shore,
So do our minutes hasten to their end;
Each changing place with that which goes before,
In sequent toil all forwards to contend.

William Shakespeare sonnet 60

I

Howling winds move off the ocean and begin to subside in a gesture of pity to those who sit huddled together in a circle along the shore. The sand soaks up the evening's rain but puddles are found where the sand has met its saturation point. The sun is steadily moving upwards pushing away clouds in its path. It will be sometime before the puddles evaporate, which leaves enough time to crash through them creating giant waterspouts over and in the jeeps and other trucks that make their way to this point on the beach.

· August mornings on our beach provides a prescription for what ails you. It isn't written into the Journal of Medicine but it could be an advertisement with sun, sand and surf that is clearly medicinal and therapeutic as well as a cleanser to the soul.

We take a walk along our shoreline stopping here and there to push away sea grass with our toes to see what can be uncovered below. Often it is the shells of discarded crabs and clams or the remnants of a seagull or tern's dinner. Our dogs are at our feet barking, hopping and jumping along with us as we investigate near the pounding surf. The wind has died down. The wind becoming still, the air getting warmer. The humidity hasn't crept its way into the air yet. Soon the ocean will be calmer and maybe the dogs will venture towards the water.

Meanwhile we walk hand in hand looking for that elusive thing. It has to be right. It has to say something to you when you find it, pick it up and examine it from all sides. The color in its brilliance will reflect the sun's morning rays. The distance we walk pales to the possibilities of finding that most elusive thing.

The smell of the salt permeates the air. There is no music here but the sounds of the waves gently pushing against the shore, than retracing its steps back into the greater ocean. Out in the distance, fishing boats trawl for fluke, flounder and out further still, swordfish, shark and tuna. Nestled amongst the fishing boats are the buoys creating a pattern around the curvature of the ocean.

She who walks with me is beautiful. She is tall, thin and has a smile that both captures and captivates you all at the same time. The breeze off the ocean gets caught in her reddish brown hair, pushing it out at once in all directions. Although it serves no purpose, she constantly runs her hand through her hair pushing it off her face until the breeze pushes it back once again.

We push west along the coast with the ocean on our left and the dunes with sharp beach grass on our right. Our walk is carefree. We leave footprints behind to show that we have trespassed on the ocean's territory. Our transgression becomes invisible as the water runs up the shoreline, erases our presence and quickly retreats among the sand, salt, rocks and silt left behind by years of crushed shells.

The remains of translucent jellyfish are intertwined with the dark green seaweed embedded into the shoreline among the crab legs, clam and mussel remains. Hidden among nature's refuse is our elusive thing. We walk as newlyweds talking about everything and talking about nothing. Our three dogs walk with us, through us, and around us. Occasionally, they will spot something at a distance and charge at it with reckless abandon. They will roll in the sand, run up to the edge of their world, but won't dare take a step into the rolling unknown.

The occasional arm of one of the ocean's most interesting and intriguing specimen, the starfish is found along our travels. It is rare to find, but when you do it offers a moment of reflection. Where is the rest of the starfish? What caused it to lose one of its appendages? How do we transfer this question to us as we ponder our lives, our past and our future? How do we react to losing pieces of us—our soul, our very being? What happens to the rest of us when we lose a piece of us?

As elusive as this is to answer, we continue to search for answers, for that is what makes us who we are. So we wander along the beach looking for the elusive thing, finding one another as we walk hand in hand on a beautiful August morning, where the sun shines brightly, warms the air, and the ocean music fills our ears with the sounds of serenity, peacefulness, comfort and joy.

By this time, many others have found their spot along the ocean. Fisherman have set up shop, placing poles in PVC piping with the line sitting far out in the water waiting for the fish to announce it's presence. Meanwhile, fisherman crack open pale beers to announce the coming of another beautiful summer morning. Resting comfortably in their beach chairs the serious and not so serious fisherman work on their lines, their tackle and bait. Others still, take out the morning paper and begin to sift through the relevant and not so relevant.

We continue to make our way across the sand being careful not to walk into the barely visible fishing line that extends some twenty yards from the shore to twenty or thirty yards into the ocean. We talk as if we have known each other all of our lives. We are best friends. We are soul mates. I never believed in soul mates until I met my best friend. She had always believed. She just hadn't found him until she met her best friend.

"What are you thinking?" she asks. To many men that is the most difficult and dreaded question that one can be asked. The answer is usually one of those elusive things. Elusive like the swordfish in Hemingway's Islands in the Stream or Melville's Moby Dick. As elusive as a scientist's reach for the smallest particles in the universe.

She believes in God and the mysteries that come forth from this belief. The very notion of this beach, the plant and sea life, the sand, the rock and dunes would be her truth of God. She believes because she needs to believe. It is important enough for her to talk about it as the miracle of the ocean stares us in the face.

My sense of the world differs in that I have no belief, no faith that all that we do, all that we sense, feel, suffer and enjoy is preordained. My miracle is scientific. My elusive thing is that I cannot put a hand on what cannot have a hand put on it. I can't see it—I can't touch it—how do you prove the existence of something that cannot be seen? Faith in the unknown and unconquerable is that elusive thing.

"I'm thinking that I love being with you for the simple things and for the complex things. This beach is both of those things—simple and complex". When we are on the beach, our universe closes in on us. There is just the two of us. There is just the sun, the water, the heat and the rhythm of the ocean. My answer results in a brief but tender kiss on the lips and the whisper of, "I love you".

The mid day sun bears down on us from directly overhead. The sounds of children playing along the water's edge add to the cacophony of people, ocean, wind, soft music and whispers. The water pours out of our pores and slides down over the oils on our skin. The smell of coconut permeates the nose as I rub extra suntan lotion on to her warm, taut, tanned skin. We can't imagine enjoying a place as much as we do this place.

There is a dance that is happening on our beach. It is a circular motion of ocean spray lifting off the oncoming wave and falling back down as the wave crests and crashes onto the shore. In this dance, children tumble and fall over one another as wave after wave lifts them, pushes them and ultimately leaves them filled with sand and laughter on the shore.

II

In the gentle breeze that comes off our ocean, that distinct smell of exhaust from the fishing boats trawling for their daily catch mixes with the friendly aroma of burning wood. Our sand pit has been dug. Charcoal mixed with dry pieces of driftwood from the dune behind us makes for a comfortable cooking fire, reminiscent of those made as a child camping out with summer camp friends.

Our lunch fire burned strong, sending wisps of smoke throughout the beach. The distinctive scent calls to us as strongly as any primitive calling inherited and captured by evolution. Our friends and neighbors with line in hand have brought the bounty of the ocean to us. With a pleasure that is unmatched by anything manmade, the fish are scaled, filleted and simply spiced. The grill top has been placed on top of our fire in the sand almost begging for the fish to be placed on its fiery surface. The sound is what we wait for. The sizzling heat; the air that is consumed immediately by the fire. The water from within the fish once saturated now slowly evaporates, as the dying hiss of heat on liquid leaves no trace of its former place.

No longer do we have the distinct odor of fishing trawlers, but the now the air is filled with the fragrance of grilled fish, rich in a bouquet of itself, butter, wine, garlic and rosemary. The sea salt mixes with the fresh squeeze of lemon. The juice of the lemon sprays out strongly at first followed by a mist as if sprayed directly into the air.

The next sound that is heard is the rush of air escaping out of our beer bottles as the opener is passed around our circle of friends. The meal is eaten quickly. Praise goes to the fisherman, the fish cleaners, the chef and most importantly, the keeper of the bottle opener.

With lunch finished, the embers of the fire dying down, it is time for the most anticipated part of the day. The unmatchable beach nap. The incessant sound of the surf ebbing in and out lulls you to sleep. Our bellies filled and our hearts content, we lay down to relax, to dream, and to sleep. And sleep on the beach comes quickly. Within minutes, you can actually feel the tension rise and leave you almost as if it were an out of body experience. Our ears are filled with the sound of the surf, of seagulls above us looking for someone's forgotten lunch, or better yet, an unwatched bag of popcorn or potato chips. All other sounds are lost and the imagination comes quickly. Peaceful dreams. Quiet dreams, unlike the dreams in a fitful sleep at home. No car chases, no guns, no danger, no work. Peaceful. Tranquil. Undisturbed. Serene.

III

Dreams. Awakenings. Reminders of things past. Elusive things. Elusive things past. Soul searching. Gentle vibrations of things to come. Imminent things. Things in the distant future. Wants and needs and the energy to obtain and attain. Things. Goals. Desires. Cravings.

I dream of boats floating out at sea. Gentle breezes capturing soft Spanish guitar playing on the boat. Gentle breezes capturing the craft and pushing it towards the harbor. In the harbor, flags are various colors; sizes and shapes are aloft over antique brick buildings. Birds singing in trees that provide shade for the natives and tourists alike in this ancient harbor town. Men and women walking along, some hand in hand, wearing white linen clothing. Off white linen. Pastels reminiscent of childhood drawings. Small coffee shops and Internet cafes line the sheets. Children running through the town under their parents' legs. Casual and carefree.

My beautiful wife, filled with happiness and energy, a smile that is radiant, sits at my side under an umbrella as we sip tea and coffee. The waiter dressed in white with black linen pants and simple black shoes brings us simple sandwiches to eat. We live here I think. It is a small harbor town in the south of Italy that we have moved to. We are exploring the simple pleasures. We explore each other. Our souls are one—has been one for sometime. We listen to the musicians sitting on a small stage in the center of the square. There is a guitar player and a flute player. Their music is suggestive of the time and place. A small town where there are no strangers. There is no crime; doors are never locked in the town or in the countryside.

Farmers come into town riding on donkeys to bring their fresh produce to market. Wagons filled with sugar beets, tomatoes, olives and of course wine grapes. Oranges, apples, potatoes and wheat and barley round out the remaining agricultural products. The wines have been spectacular. We particularly enjoy the reds whether in our cottage or out to dinner along the walkway in the center of town.

After dinner, we typically drive out to the countryside to watch the sun set. I love watching how the wind blows through my beautiful wife's hair as we run the curves in our convertible. The smells are different out in the countryside. The wind dies down the further away we drive from the shoreline. I reach across after shifting into fifth gear to run my hands through her long, what I would call, auburn hair. (She may not agree). She turns and smiles with that knowing look. We know that we have always been meant to be; it was a matter of, in her words, *fate* to intervene.

We find our spot—the ciffside area that looks over the hills and valleys that provides us with the best review of the setting sun. On our blanket, we have cheese spreads with meats and crackers. I slowly uncork a bottle of cabernet sauvignon and set it aside to breathe. She pulls two wine glasses from a pouch and sets it down near the bottle. The light from the sun streams through the bottle and cascades a brilliant red and orange along our blanket.

Using the pouch as a pillow, I laid my head back. She laid her head down on my chest and smiled. She closed her eyes as she hugged me tightly. We enjoyed the peacefulness together.

Our cottage, which sits on a pond, is small. The fireplace in the living room is made of stone and faces out on two sides. The fireplace faces the kitchen on the other side where we spend a great deal of time cooking and entertaining our small group of friends. It has taken some time, but our knowledge of Italian is growing and we are able to converse with some confidence. My wife has begun to think in Italian but I haven't been able to grasp that concept yet. She is more than capable of filling in for my small handicap.

Our porch is a wrap around porch where we spend mornings reading the English language newspapers and having coffee and breakfast. The porch and railings have been whitewashed. It complements the pale blue of the house's exterior. Surrounding the house are acres of untamed land. Grass grows freely in areas, but diminishes, as it gets closer to the pond. At the pond sits a small wooden rowboat that we use from time to time. Mostly it sits because it looks like a picture I had once purchased from IKEA. Closer to the house are a variety of trees, some fruit producing, others not. The dogs run free but the closest they will get to the water is sitting in the rowboat.

She slept on the ride home after our viewing of the sunset. We drove down the dirt path that leads from the road up to our cottage. The dirt road is tree lined and has small solar powered lanterns in the ground every twenty yards or so. I kissed her gently and she stirred. "Come on honey. We're home." We walked up the creaky wooden steps of our home. The dogs greeted us and ran out to do their business.

We walked through the living room into the kitchen and dropped off the empty wine bottle, the used glasses with the wine stain on the bottom and the empty containers with the knives wrapped in napkins. "Honey, this is going to wait until tomorrow." "Great idea," she replied. "Why don't you come upstairs? I think we should make love." She took me by the hand and we walked across the room to the circular stairs that led to a tremendous bedroom. The bedroom was the only room upstairs and it too had a wraparound porch with windows filling out the perimeter. In it are two rustic red loveseats with a small dark wood table to set down our books and coffee cups while we read. We lit some candles, turned on soft jazz and looked each other in the eyes before falling into one another's arms in bed.

IV

I felt a bead of sweat form on my forehead and slowly fall into my left eye. As I moved my hand to wipe it I realized my dream was over and I was awakening to a blazing sun on the beach. It took a moment, but I raised myself from the lounge chair and shook off the sleep and ambled down to the water to cool off. It wasn't far to go. While I slept the tide came closer to where we sat. The sun was no longer overhead but at an angle where I guessed it must have been around 3:00.

She left our friends and joined me a few minutes later in the water. She rode on my back as I swam parallel to the shoreline. The water was cool and refreshing. I turned around and dropped her off my back. She laughed and splashed water in my face. I leaped at her, picking her up and throwing her across my shoulder and dropping her down into the surf. She spit up water and thrust herself at me trying to push me down. It was Einstein, or Newton or some other scientific genius that wrote a treatise about inertia or kinetic energy. The bottom line is that an object that weights 115 pounds is not moving an object that weighs 225 pounds. It is simply a fact of physics.

After toweling off, we sat together with a beer and began to discuss tonight's menu at our restaurant, Katie's Place. After retiring we decided to open a restaurant because I enjoyed cooking and she loved talking to people. Any people and about anything. Since it was to be her face out there each evening, we decided to name it after her. After being in the limelight for so many years in my prior career, I had no hesitation about hiding in the back with the grease, the jazz, the clanging of pots and pans and sizzling of things on the stove. It had become my new music.

Norah Jones plays in the background as she makes her way through the throngs of customers sipping wine at the bar waiting for a table to open up. The well manicured, the coiffed and the cologne wearers blend together in laughter and small talk. Bodies slide by one another, some innocently and some not so. Human beings have a need to touch, to feel close, to hold and to grasp. To have contact. To find that elusive thing.

She is wearing black jeans, pink cowboy boots and a pink button down shirt from Ralph Loren. She sidles up to customers asking about their families. About their day. About their shoes. From there she and her customers become best of friends. They become our repeat offenders. Typically they will order the same type of drinks and the same dinners, but sometimes become daring enough to try the new items on the menu that I dreamed about while on the beach.

This evening the two specials are Italian based. The first is veal dredged in flower wrapped around spinach, two cheeses, sage, spices and sautéed in butter, olive oil and white wine. It is served with rice pilaf on the side. The second special is monkfish, also dredged in flower and sautéed. It is served with a sauce made of red wine, a basic tomato sauce, arugala, butter, salt and pepper, fresh garlic and fresh rosemary. It is finished off with fresh chopped parsley. Pasta is the side dish with tomato sauce.

At some point in the evening I make my way out to the dining room to say hello to my wife and speak to the patrons. To some I speak of the chances of the local sports teams, to others local politics and to others fine wines and bourbons. I stay long enough to be welcoming and friendly, but not long enough to be uncomfortable. I find my way back to the kitchen where the redolence of garlic permeates and the comfortable routine of preparing and cooking.

I let Katie deal with the waiters and waitresses. The image that they front is the image of Katie's Place. There is neither time nor place for the cattiness that may be the interchanges between waitresses. If you have an opinion about a customer, she expects you to keep it to yourself as long as there are any customers in the restaurant.

It is hard not to pick up on the myriad conversations at each of the tables. It is the sound of relationships and the human condition. Each of the tables has its very own story. The story of the push and pull of a relationship amongst the seated guests. The greater the party, the less intimate the conversations. The intimate conversations are delayed and spoken of in the ladies room. These are the things the men know nothing about. These are the tug of war issues each relationship has. These are the conversations amongst close allies typically over the telephone while drinking a glass of wine. The needs and wants. The things their husbands don't understand or don't want to understand or make sense of. Their elusive things.

Men on the other hand are strong and can weather any storm. We maintain the balancing act in our hearts and heads and keep our emotions in check. We are not discussing our elusive things out in public. Each man at the table has an elusive thing, but it is their elusive thing and has to be worked out on their own and in their own time and fashion. Or so we think. Each of the men at the table has their own poison and demons and remedies for them. One hides in a bottle of scotch, one swallows anti-depressants like lifesavers while another is a few blood pressure points away from his heart attack. Brave, insular, a self-secure but frightened child who like many of us won't ask for directions even though there is a service station on all four corners of the crossroads where we sit, stalled in a decision with horns blaring behind us with warnings and intentions.

At another table, an intimate dialog between two young lovers ensues. They discuss everything. There are no secrets. There is full disclosure without censorship. They barely touch their food. They enjoyed what they ate but are enjoying each other's eyes. They are locked in a myopic tunnel vision. They are mesmerized by each detail, by each word, each whisper, and each shift of the body. The body language tells their story from a distance. They talk about where they are going to do it next. Which exciting place with the chance of being seen. It thrills them. Their temperatures rise and faces flush with excitement. They ask for the check and can't pay it fast enough.

By eleven o'clock we head out to the parking lot and make the short drive home. The busboys and waitresses have cleaned up the tables and counters. The side work has been completed; the condiment containers are all refilled and cleaned. The menus are cleaned as well. The cleaning crew will be in the next morning to prepare the restaurant for another evening of people looking, talking, listening, ignoring, plotting, sabotaging, and falling in love again for the first time, for the last time.

* * *

After packing our things in the back of the jeep, the three dogs tentatively jump in and find a spot amongst the beach paraphernalia. In four-wheel low, we crawl over some rocks and through sand dunes until we make it to a reasonably passable stretch of sand and rocks and shift it into four-wheel high until we get to pavement where four-wheel drive is no longer necessary. The sounds of the water fade into the background and the sound of cars passing takes its place. The top is open and we drive at a good pace. The sun is much more comfortable at 60 miles per hour. The dogs with their tongues hanging out of open mouths enjoy the rush of air moving on their faces.

Our silence in the car means nothing. We are happy and content with each other and the simple gestures while driving is conversation enough. We didn't find our elusive thing today, but we have many tomorrows.

V

John slipped a tranquilizer out of his pocket and put it in his mouth. He had been taking these daily serenity pills for some time now. It seemed to take the edge off his daily grind in and out of the city. He made his way onto the Long Island Railroad and as he had become accustomed to, he stood against the doorway reading the morning paper.

The train moved quickly, but not quickly enough to quell the growing uneasiness in his stomach. He felt the usual claustrophobia creeping over him like a snake slithers before its prey ready to pounce with its venomous fangs. Driving was no better; especially sitting in bumper-to-bumper traffic on any of the three nightmares they called parkways or expressways. The Southern State, though picturesque was ugly, the Northern state faired no better and the Long Island Expressway was simply downright hostile.

His time as an investment banker has taken him through some interesting peaks and valleys. At fifty-three years old, he has married and divorced three times, having none of his own children in any of the marriages, but having two stepchildren from his second wife. He still looks remarkably handsome. His three pieces suits, either black or grey with crisp white shirts and matching ties, attract women of all ages. Although silver, his hair is thick and on the longish side worn slicked back with gel. His black-framed glasses accentuate the already intelligent look that makes women notice him. He is fit and stands at 6 feet, 2 inches tall, obviously one who takes whatever down time he has and works out at the gym.

It is in the gym where he first realized the onset of emotional challenges. He began to find himself turning inward, being retrospective and asking himself questions. Exacerbating the problem was the fact that he didn't particularly care for his answers nor were any better answers or solutions forthcoming. He tried to ignore these difficulties but that was neither his style nor his personality. With a type A personality on Wall Street, these are not the typical personality traits. He began to work late at the office to avoid the train ride home and the empty house. Meals were sporadic. He ventured out to restaurants on his own but felt uncomfortable. He tried skipping meals but that didn't help him at the gym.

One evening, another gym rat was running alongside him on a treadmill. They didn't know each other's name but recognized each other from frequent visits to the gym and as a result gave the cursory nod or a quick "how ya doin" when passing each other in an aisle. Today, Ron an overweight and overworked truck driver looked over and said, "I don't mean to pry, but…who are you running from?" John slowed the treadmill until he began to walk. He draped the towel that was in front of him on the handlebars over his shoulder. He wiped his face, let out a long burst of air and looked at Ron. "You know what? I haven't quite figured that out yet. It is eluding the fuck out of me". He paused and looked up at the television above the row of treadmills. It was CNBC and the ticker was running below it. The ticker knew where it was coming from and where it was going. It had no goals, no agenda, and no predetermined notions. It answered to no one and was responsible to no one. It just was. John looked back at his questioner. "Gotta take a shower. Take care."

He towels off and admires himself in the mirror. He dissects himself in the mirror as well and as the adrenaline begins to dissipate, the doubts and self-analysis once again begins to take over. The self—administered recriminations begin to fester and the thinking and self-absorption replace the adrenaline rush. He walks to his locker, opens it and takes out a pill from a bottle in his gym bag. He looks at the label on the prescription bottle and notes that it warns against taking this medication with alcohol.

Hasn't stopped him before—hasn't harmed him before. He studies the orange—rust colored container for another moment and decides to take two more pills out. If he hesitates he knows he won't take them. So he doesn't hesitate. He swallows all three and flushes them down with the remaining Gatorade from his workout.

He dresses slowly, combs his hair and gathers up his belongings. In one hand is his gym bag with its soggy clothes and in his other is his suit and shirt from the day. As he heads out of the locker room into the rush of air-conditioned air in the gym, he takes a sweeping look of the place. He doesn't think that he will be returning here. His mind is fraught with too much despair. He wants to drink. He wants to drink and drive. He wants to drown out the voices in his head. He wants to drown out the noise with the surf at the beach. He wants to drown. He will accomplish all of this tonight.

When they find him face down on the sand hours later when the dawn burst through the clouds, he had a poem in his pocket. It was handwritten, much of the ink disappearing in the turmoil of the churning ocean. But it was both recognizable and readable.

> Take this kiss upon thy brow
> And, in parting from you now,
> Thus much let me avow-
> You are not wrong, to deem
> That my days here have been a dream;
> Yet if hope has flown away
> In a night, or in a day,
> In a vision, or in none,
> Is it therefore the less gone?
> All that we see or seem
> Is but a dream within a dream
> I stand amid the roar
> Of a surf tormented shore,
> And I hold within my hand
> Grains of the golden sand—
> How few! Yet how they creep

Through my fingers of the deep,
While I weep—while I weep!
O God! Can I not grasp
Them with a tighter clasp?
O God! Can I not save
One from the pitiless wave?
Is all that we see or seem
But a dream within a dream?

The officer in charge began taking statements from the runners who had discovered the body. It didn't look like much at first from a distance as it had been covered in what looked like mounds of spinach. The two runners had noticed hands and a shoe protruding from the seaweed and after a moments hesitation, pulled the tangled green mass off the body. There was nothing more to be gained so he let the women, clearly shocked and affected by their discovery, go.

The officer, a twelve year veteran had seen his share of drowned and bloated bodies floating in streams, harbors and of course the ocean. Drowning was common, suicides were common and it didn't matter the socioeconomic class. It harbored no feelings one-way or the other. Water was master over man. Water needed to be conquered by man. Rafts, rowboats, dugout canoes, 15th century sailing vessels to tame the wild oceans and explore lands and peoples separated by its great breadth, depth and spirit.

Powered by man, by steam, by coal or other fossil fuel or by nuclear power, the sea going man lived to tell of his travels in pursuing one venture or another. Pursuing one's elusive dreams over millennia still left the ocean as master and man as slave to its power over him and the strength of spirit to break him.

Detective Bill Ranson had just touched down last night with his family after a vacation in the Dominican Republic. Ranson was fit and restless. He had become more thoughtful. He felt he was becoming more complex, thinking more. Thinking more about the human condition. He was also becoming more cynical, but that came with the job. But when he wasn't working he was always noticing. He was always looking, creating snapshots of the world going by in his head. This too was not just a reflection of his job, but more of who he was becoming. As he got older, he became more philosophical. He read more and was thinking himself well read.

The Dominican Republic was an eye opener for him, his wife and two kids, both boys. He and his wife needed this vacation. His job as a detective was consuming him and his wife's legal career too, was becoming taxing on the family. The brochures were beautiful, the amenities were beautiful and the sand was white, with tall thin trees sprouting here and there along the intoxicating coastline.

Everything was wonderful and breathtaking if you were an American tourist, or a European or Russian tourist. Your capitalism and place in your respective social system allowed you to visit this far off tropical paradise. As warned, the tropical paradise did not extend past the armed guards of the hotel's perimeter.

The bus ride to the resort led them through stark poverty. Homes were nothing more than shacks along a dirty road fenced in by wire posts. Helmet less men and boys rode motor scooters along the road and off the road. Many of these scooters were nothing more than improvised taxis that transported people to and from dirty destinations.

Ranson couldn't help but wonder about the human condition here. The crime, the absence of light in a brightly lit island. The farm animals were emaciated. "The cows have ribcages," his eight year old, Ricky yelled out for all to hear on the bus. There were little chuckles of recognition, but for the sake of the bus driver, nobody wanted to mention what was so readily apparent to anyone with a conscience. Boards of directors, their CEOs and CFOs and shareholders are the venture capitalists that gain from an influx of money—the impoverished continue to be impoverished. The impact is limited to the few who are wise enough and have the aptitude to work in the resort industry on their own island. The elusive dollar hasn't trickled down to the barefoot children on this island split between two countries, the Dominican Republic and Haiti. The human condition here continues in spite of capitalism. Or he thinks, is it the other way around?

He thinks that the human condition may be a mental state. After all, the dead body on the beach appears by all indication to have money. His car, a silver Infiniti holds a fine suit and an expensive leather briefcase along with a laptop. His team has already determined the identity of their D.B. John Sizemore, 53, a Wall Street banker who lives alone in a small Suffolk County town. An autopsy and the forensics unit will gather up more useful information so that he can begin his investigation.

Ranson looks over to his partner, a husky cigar smoking twenty-two year vet whose raspy voice reminds him of some cartoon he watched as a child. He thinks he needs to drop a few pounds and cut down on the booze and maybe he will live a couple of years past his retirement, which he plans to do in a year or so. Ranson looks into the vast ocean. The water color isn't the same as the water color closer to the equator. The sand is lighter as well. But this is his ocean. He is comfortable here. It tells stories to him. He wonders how much of John Sizemore's story is intertwined with the Atlantic.

Ranson and his oversized partner, Frank Tinney head back to the precinct to do some background work on the dead body. Tinney looks up the name in the computer and waits for any hits to come up. He looks through the wallet and pulls out credit cards and begins to make some investigative phone calls. Where does he spend his money? What were the last purchases? Where does he like to eat, what does he like to drink? What skeletons will come falling out of the closet?

Ranson is more interested in the poem. He Googles the first few line of the poem, *take this kiss upon thy brow!* It didn't take long to see that is an Edgar Allan Poe poem and after a few clicks, the entire poem was printed out and sitting before him. Out loud, but to no one in particular, "Okay, Mr. Sizemore, what does this have to do with finding you dead on the beach?"

A few more clicks and he was on Wikipedia looking into the life and death of Mr. Poe. Ranson begins taking notes on a pad that he takes out of the draw of his old, worn out and scratched up wooden desk. His notes are bulleted and in order of what he has read.

Poe

Depression, madness
Drinking—erratic behavior
Court martial for disobedience
Foster child with aunt and uncle—estranged from uncle
Virginia—cousin—gets sick—Poe upset—drinking
Death
Delirious
Incoherent for days
Not wearing his own clothes when found
Poe's poems—single aesthetic experience—Could be important
Allegory—conveying a meaning that is other than literal—can be
writing or art

Ranson looks over to Tinney. "You get the tox report yet?"

"Another half-hour or so. Our guy likes to eat out a lot. A restaurant called Katie's Place. You been there?"

"Not yet. Heard good things about it. Hungry?"

Tinney rubs his oversized belly and smiles. "What do you think? I'll see what time they open. I could use a new place anyway. Then we should go hit Sizemore's gym."

"Good. Maybe you can lift something when we're over there," he says sarcastically.

"Yeah! And, maybe you can lift this!" He lifts his right hand in the air and slowly unleashes his middle finger.

VI

She steps into the kitchen and walks over to her husband and gently places a kiss on his lips. "What was that for?" he asks. "That was for nothing. Now get to work". And with that she slaps him on the butt, turns quickly and walks back into the restaurant proper. He feels a lot of energy this evening. He circles his thumb through his IPOD and finds just what is needed. The Essential Earth Wind and Fire. The first three songs on there own get him going through the pre-dinner workout. Cutting, slicing, dicing, chopping, washing and pounding. September, Serpentine Fire and Fantasy. He feels it in his bones—a great way to start the evening—that and a nice French Bordeaux. He and his souse chefs are dancing and grooving through the kitchen. The waiters and waitresses look through the window and laugh. Katie sneaks up to the window and smiles. This is everything that they ever wanted. The bus boys sneak in and grab ladles and spoons and start banging on the overhead pots and pans. Pretty soon the bartender turns the speaker on from the kitchen and blasts it into the empty restaurant. By this time, Written in Stone is on and everyone is dancing around, placing napkins and silverware on tables, making spin moves with water bottles, placing apples and lemons in the water carafes.

Listening to EW&F he decides tonight's specials will be BBQ ribs, chicken and fillet of sole, which he will try to convince Katie to write on the board as Fillet of Soul. The specials he created at the beach today will wait for another night. To him, music is one of those things that is not elusive. As a sax player, he could bury his day and open his passions and let his fingers and mouth be his emotional sounding board. His professional day would slip away like sand on the beach, finding a new home every second as the water turned over and over. Within a half hour of playing, the day fell away like an onion's layers are peeled away, piece-by-piece until there was nothing but the music. No distractions. No other sounds but his performing along with the IPOD. This is as therapeutic as the surf running in his ears as he sleeps on the beach.

Katie moved around the restaurant floor like a dancer on a stage. She was graceful, turning here to laugh with a customer or playing to a table like a Catskill lounge singer. She was able to bring that intangible something to her guests that you couldn't really put your finger on. Whatever it was, it had charm and appeal and it brought customers back frequently. (And dinner wasn't bad either).

She moved over to a table that sat two men whom she had never seen before. They had paperwork before them and although they tried to be discreet, their voices were overpowering.

"How is everything here tonight?" she asked.

Tinney looked up and smiled. "The food is great. I'm not a jazz fan, but I can learn to adapt".

"Yes, my friend here is evolving", Ranson chimed in. "Since you're here", he continued, "Have you ever seen this man here before?" He took out a picture and passed it over to Katie.

"John? He's a regular. Is he in trouble?"

"I'm sorry to tell you, but he was found on the beach this morning. He drowned," Ranson said.

"Oh my God! What happened? Can you talk about it?"

"Well, that is why we are here—and to try out the food".

"Nothing like tact, Tinney".

"I need something to drink", she decided. "What are you guys having?"

Katie spent the next thirty minutes sitting with the detectives and talking about John Sizemore. Although she knew about most of her customers, she happened to know a great deal more about John. One of her waitresses had been seeing him on and off for sometime.

"He liked his bourbon. He could handle it. We never needed to cut him off or anything. He liked to come here and unwind. Every now and then my husband…he's the chef here, would come out and they would discuss music and politics and any of their other boring nerdy stuff".

"I take it you had no interest in the nerdy stuff?" Ranson asked.

"Are you kidding? I would rather talk about shoes with my customers. That doesn't make me shallow, but after listening to the two of them, or my husband with any of the guys, I'd rather have a drink with the girls and keep things light".

Tinney asked about his waitress girlfriend. Her name was Christine and she wasn't working tonight. Christine was working her way through graduate school, trying to get her MBA. She worked in the city Monday through Friday, but spent Friday and Saturday nights here at the restaurant.

"Could you tell me anything about their relationship?" Ranson asked.

"I could, but that would make me a gossip. I don't do gossip".

"No, you do shoes".

"I do shoes. I can give you her number if you like. Listen, I need to get back to my customers. Enjoy your dinner. The drinks are on the house. Could you let me know what happened?"

Tinney responded. "You don't do gossip."

"Touché", she said in response, and began walking through the throng of tables.

The two detectives watched her walk away. They smiled at each other knowing what the other was thinking. "Looks good", Tinney said. "Food's not bad either", Ranson replied.

They finished their dinner, paid their bill and walked out into the humid summer evening. The car was parked in the back of the lot, so Tinney grabbed a quick cigarette before getting to the car.

"So what do you think?" Tinney asked of his partner.

"Let's get acquainted with the waitress and see what we get from her. Then we can head back and see what forensics has for us. They got into Sizemore's house so we should have a decent profile".

"I'm curious to know about his drinking and pill popping. His toxicology was off the freakin' charts. Maybe our little waitress was playing pharmacologist".

They drove silently the thirty minutes it took to reach Christine Montero's apartment. She lived on the ground level floor of a two family house. Whether it was a legal two family or not they couldn't say nor did they care.

The house was a split ranch with an extension. It had brown shingles with white windows and matching trim. The grass was well manicured and the landscaping was impeccable. There was a rock garden on the north side of the house, which when lit up with solar lighting on the ground gave off a cascade of shadows. There were two maples in front of the house on either side of the driveway. On the property itself, were two Japanese Maples, obviously expensive, rich in red coloring and neatly trimmed. A bed of soil mixed with various perennials made up the perimeter of the house. The house was clearly well maintained, which had nothing to do with the waitress, and all to do with her landlord.

As it turned out, her landlord was her mother. Tough times on Long Island. High taxes, high costs, skyrocketing housing costs. The kids are all coming home after college and staying there well into their twenties trying to make a niche for themselves.

Christine opened the door after two rings. They showed their badges, but she was still reluctant to let them in. It took some time to convince her that they were really police officers. I suppose they couldn't blame her— times have changed when you really have to prove who you are to the public. Better safe than sorry as the saying goes.

She let them in hesitantly and quickly apologized for the disorder. She explained that she works long hours and hadn't gotten around to straightening up yet. They told her not to worry. She still was a "doubting Thomas" when she asked, "Why are you here? What is this about?"

Christine was a beautiful young woman. She stood at about 5 foot 6 inches with a slender frame, bluish eyes and blond hair. Neither detective doubted why John Sizemore was attracted to her.

"You might want to sit down", Ranson suggested. She began to grow pale as if the words themselves were a death sentence. She sat at the dining room table where she had been finishing a salad. She appeared to be working on some financial charts on her laptop, which sat just to the right of her dinner plate. On the left, was an open briefcase with several multi-colored folders.

"Its about John Sizemore", Ranson began.

"What about him? Is he alright? What's going on?" She blurted one quick question off after another.

"I am truly sorry, but he was found on the beach this morning. He drowned". He waited for this to sink in and both he and Tinney observed her reaction.

"What do you mean he drowned? He's a great swimmer". She paused. To herself and to her guests, she asked, "What was he doing at the beach?" She began to cry. "I have to see him. Where is he! I have to see him!" She stood up to get her jacket from the closet.

"We need to ask you a few questions first and then we can take you to see him", Tinney tactfully told her. "We believe it was a suicide".

She closed her eyes and the tears began to trickle down slowly at first, and then as the realization and the impact of the news, the tears came stronger. "Can we go and talk at the same time? Oh my God, John, what happened to you? What have you done?" Her face grew paler and her expression dark. She tried to stand up, but fell short of her goal, falling face first into Ranson. He carried her limp body to the couch and laid her down. Tinney went to the bathroom and brought back a cold, damp towel and placed it on her forehead after wiping her face. It didn't take long before she was conscious again.

VII

We drove home quietly after closing up the restaurant. Katie filled me in on her conversation with the two detectives. We both liked John very much. We liked Christine as well. She was like a daughter to us especially after she had lost her father two years earlier. While she wasn't looking for a replacement family, it was evident that she needed to speak to someone. She needed someone to bounce ideas off of. She needed to feel as a part of something. Although she was somewhat close to her mother, it wasn't enough and it didn't serve her needs. Sizemore, a professional, a bright and articulate man with a great many things to offer, stepped into the role agreeably.

Katie knew when I needed to be alone. She knew my telltale signs; the sullen face, the dark cloud enclosing me, and she let me be. I grabbed a glass and opened up a bottle of bourbon. I went into the den, keeping the lights off and turned on ESPN. Baseball Tonight was running the Top Ten highlights but I was looking at the crawl at the bottom. "Damn!" Perfect way to cap off a crappy night. The Mets lost and those freaking Yankees won. I won't tell Katie. She'll just gloat or do some stupid dance about her two hunks, A-Rod and Jeter. It's enough to make you sick.

"You say something, honey?"

"No. Just spilled my drink. I'll be up shortly".

But it was more than that. John's death put me into a grey stupor. Visions danced across my eyes. Visions of darkness, despair; an abyss of despair. That would happen now and then and a dank mood would envelope me. For me that meant headphones and my sax or inventing something on the piano. Katie liked to listen to me play the piano—she also knew that when I did I had issues to deal with, clouds to part and a hole to fill.

I felt somewhat guilty in what I knew. I knew that John was going through a lot. There was a spirit about him that worked as strongly as the force of a magnet. Each of us had a darkness about us that could come at anytime. We became friendly after he started coming to the restaurant earlier and earlier. I didn't mind. He would come in back while I prepared for the dinner crowd. We talked about work on Wall Street. We talked about my life prior to retirement. He spoke more about himself than I did about myself. We both shared a passion for bourbon.

I remember one night in late fall when we took the train to the city for the Annual Whiskey Fest. It was an evening of wine tasting without the wine. Fine bourbons all night. The food that was served throughout the evening was more about staying somewhat sober rather than the culinary delights in of itself. After a while, it was one piece of bread to follow three or four bourbons. It was that night that he told me of his need to write. He wanted to be a prolific writer. He wanted to leave something behind of value to whoever may want it. Whoever may want to read it. Whoever may want to learn something from his pain. He wanted it to be read as a ripple of hope, but knew it would be an abyss of despair. That's where I got the phrase from—An Abyss of Despair. It was lyrical. It was poignant and powerful. I never sat down to read it. Frankly, I was afraid of it. I was afraid after listening to him speak that I would be drawn into his pain and isolation. I wasn't prepared to do that. I had had my own train wrecks to tow away and start fresh from. But if there was a time that I would be ready for it, it would be tonight.

I walked across the house to my desk and retrieved his manuscript. It was entitled 6112. It held no meaning for me, but his death hadn't either. I stopped into the kitchen to pick up a bottle of Maker's Mark. I walked back into the den and put on the IPOD, circling to Miles Davis. I made myself comfortable on the couch, put the pillows under my head and waited for the dogs to jump up and find their spots. One on my legs, one above my head on the pillow and the third near my side. I waited for each of them to let out a heavy breath. This meant that they were comfortable and I could begin to read. I had the sense that I was going to feel guilty for not reading this earlier. Like five weeks ago when he gave it to me. I just hadn't found the time to do so. No that isn't quite true. I had the time. I was afraid of what I might find. I pulled his manuscript out of a manila folder and began to read.

So how does one come to terms with changes in life, whether fragmented over time or a complete overturning of the mind, soul and spirit? Do you wake up one morning in a beautiful, yet modest home with a wife and try to make sense of your life or come to terms with what that life is or represents or even means? Time can be a painful reminder of what could be, should be or what may never be. So I sit here in the dark wearing comfortable pajama bottoms bought with money when money finally became a non-issue after spending so long to reach that ability to spend without thinking too much into the actual purchase.

Our house sits on an over sized property lot. Two acres of grass, shrubs and colorful trees to shade us from the summer's heat. The exterior of the house is a soft yellow vinyl in both diagonal and vertical lines accented by plants that twirl into itself, while others seem to almost have steps to climb to it's peak. There were simple apple trees and bushes that opened up into beautiful flowers that attracted bees in the spring and summer. Walking through the house one would imagine we were transplants of an earlier time. Antiques and early American pieces adorned the walls and pictures of her children filled the walls and along the staircase as you made your way upstairs to the bedrooms.

The house was our home, it was everything that we represented, it was everything that we had built together, but it was both empty and hollow. The house was rich and alive, but I felt alone and isolated. Again. Did I mention that this was wife number three? Everything I needed and wanted was here but I was emotionally bankrupt. So begins a tale that is painful and frightening. A tale that I write for you while sitting in my pajamas in the dark in a room that pales in comparison to a jail cell. Outside of my window is a deserted parking lot that sits adjacent to the local rail line. It is quiet now except for the occasional car that drives by or the passenger trains that come by every now and then. Although the television is on, mostly for light and company, it is muted at the moment; the only other sound appears to be the snoring of a gentleman that has a jail cell next to mine. It really isn't as bad as it sounds. It is my little hovel as I have come to affectionately name it.

Aside from the lyrics that I have written all to infrequently, this is the first real attempt at verbalizing my emotions in this format. Frankly, it is one of the first real attempts at verbalizing my emotions in any format. When I did write lyrics, they were emotional outpourings. They dealt with relationships and love in somewhat of a surreal way. It was ramblings and rhymes in themes, in narrative and in prose and typically with the use of metaphors. I guess this way I didn't really say what I meant or maybe I just wanted it to sound better, more intellectual.

When did I begin to question the meaning of life and what was in store for me? I have both lost and found my direction and I haven't quite come to terms or to grips with it as of yet, but my new accommodations will more than likely help me to gather up the data, process it and still be as confounded as I was all along. I used to be quite grounded. I had a purpose and I had a direction. I think I did anyway, perhaps that isn't quite as accurate as I would profess it to be. I have questioned myself and analyzed everything I have ever done. I would try to deal with reality and within the bigger picture and then question my ability to make it succeed. I don't quite know if I am making any type of sense now. As you can see by my writing, I write and sometimes speak tangentially. I think the biggest question that I ask is that of satisfaction. When is enough, enough?

I have just spent a page and a half writing about shit. I haven't developed any characters, I haven't discussed plot. It seems somewhat disjointed and without focus. I suppose

that is the point at the moment. The questions have been there for years, the roller coaster and ensuing ride through modern day Beirut replete with landmines and cannon fire has been for a year. I'm back to metaphors. It would probably be a good idea to go to sleep right about now. There is nothing like listening to CNN to help you put your mind at ease and put your life in perspective. But sometimes a little self-indulgence and reflection go along way in attacking issues central to the theme. Have I developed a theme yet or have I just taken you on a journey in tangentially. Quite frankly, aside from myself, I am not quite sure anyone will be reading this exercise whether by my choice or theirs. The word tangentially has a nice flow. It slides off the tongue like silk on the skin of a beautiful woman. Now there's a nice simile.

I don't have a place to hang up my coats. They sit helplessly on each corner of the flimsy doors to my holder of clothes. It stands just a few inches higher than my six-foot two-inch frame. It is nice enough; it will hold most of my clothes, as long as I leave most of them home. I suppose beggars can't be choosers. That's what I told the landlord of my humble hovel.

It's just as well. For 150 bucks per week, I should be happy that I will have some money in my pocket at the end of the day. My tale is mine, so I will tell it as I will, but don't misinterpret my meaning. This isn't Les Mis; I wasn't born into my situation; I created, developed and orchestrated my own theatrical event. Maybe if I turn this into a musical, the lyrics will come in handy. I'll ask Elton John to write the music. He bears some measure (no pun intended, but it is nice that it works itself in well here) of responsibility to all of this. Not his per se, but musical lyrics have a way of creeping into your mind and altering your direction.

Nearly an hour into writing and the closing of a second page and I have not examined the characters in this story, except for myself. Funny, my wife (my third, by the way—that in itself gives insight into my life) just this evening mentioned that it is always about me. Perhaps I will turn in now and write about the other characters in this chapter of my life. Hell, if I want to write about nothing more than just myself, who cares? It is my computer and my time. I will do with it as I see fit. Fit is actually a good segue into my two main characters. How do they fit into the drama being unfolded here? And now that the drama is unfolding, where does it go from here? Fantasyland is no longer an option anymore. This is reality, like it or not.

I am into my second night as a resident of the hovel. It is after eleven in the evening and I have the feeling that sleep won't be coming anytime soon. I also have the feeling that ideas won't be flowing as easily as they did last evening. I think at some point I will begin to take the sounds of the Long Island railroad, my next-door neighbor, for granted. There is something to be said for the quiet and solitude of my room. The walls are bare and painted a bright white. The quiet and solitude has been broken yet again by my rolling neighbor. Perhaps getting used to the steel thunder was somewhat premature, but once again the quiet and serenity has returned. Serenity is probably too strong a word as that feeling has eluded me for some time. Serenity belongs in a meadow with acres of tall grass intertwined with bright daisies and sunflower plants. Serenity is probably an exercise in futility and one that escapes most of the earth's inhabitants.

I am not getting very far tonight. It seems forced and contrived rather than words and phrases, bits of emotional meaning that leaps at the page through my fingertips. That was pretty honest. Honesty is something that is learned, something that is painful, something that can have the ability to free you of burdens and unmentionable weight. Reneging on my responsibility to be honest has led to feelings of despair and chaos. These feelings have impacted the lives of others around me whether they knew it or not. These feelings led to an emptiness and darkness only surpassed by the words of talented literary artists of horror. Nonetheless, these literary artists used their passion, talent and energy to create images of horror while I created my own personal horror feature film by withholding words, passion and energy.

It is funny how perspectives change when you hear the terms depression and your name linked in the same sentence. It is equally amusing to hear professionals question you about things that you have questioned yourself that you have always found odd. Simple things like making sure if the right side of you did something, the left had to do the same to keep it even. Shaving starting on the same side each time or putting on the right shoe first rather than the left—to keep the routine was imperative.

I love cufflinks; they tell something about the person; they need to match certain types of clothing or events and most importantly, they need to be placed in the exact same location next to the other cufflinks after they are worn each day. Same with ties. The tie makes the outfit that much more professional. But they too need to be put back in order. Color order. You learn these things about yourself and that labels are attached to them.

Depression certainly affects your day-to-day movements. It drains you of any energy that you may have. Any chance to close your eyes and dismiss the world around you is a welcome relief—much like my hovel. There is nobody here to deal with except my own thoughts and quite frankly, that isn't always the most fortuitous thing. Did I put my name on top of the paper like a school child? I am John Sizemore, an investment banker on Wall Street.

Music is mind altering and mood altering. Music can be stirring and violent. It conjures up images and emotions like no other stimulant. It is powerful enough to encourage you to inch your mode of transportation ever so closely to the line and then over the line so that screams of twisted metal and concrete drown out the sounds in your own head. It could inch you ever closer to the eighteen-wheeler up ahead coming at you with enough inertia to move you backwards in one final crushing blow. There never was any conclusion to these fantastic daydreams. There was never pain nor was there ever any blood. I am not quite sure there was finality, just a reassurance that it was a possibility. Thanksgiving was especially fulfilling this year. I was thankful to the intellect, to the dedication and drive of those who create a witches brew that eases the mind and it's suffering. Thank god for anti-depressants. It has given me back a sense of myself and who I am. The tranquilizers certainly were an integral component in creating a sense of well being, the many nosedives not withstanding. It didn't take much to crash and lose that sense of well-being. It did however; take much longer to get the wheels back on track. That last phrase probably came from the fact that the silence was once again *broken by the sounds of my neighbor. It is obviously getting late as my neighbor comes by less frequently as the night wares on.*

Your author is masterfully using task avoidance this evening, a technique enjoyed by children to get out of doing something they don't like. I seem to be avoiding the character development portion of this narrative. Perhaps tomorrow evening. Perhaps this particular writing needs an incentive. Perhaps a martini to help focus on that which is being ignored. It goes back to being able to verbalize the truth, for the truth shall set you free. It is what has brought me to the hovel. The hovel isn't necessarily a bad thing, though. I am placed in a position where the worst is over, in my mind anyway. I don't know enough about the position that I am in to determine where I am in the process and if in fact the worst is over. What happens next and how long does next take before it gets here? Am I in a rush to have next come or should I be using this time to get a sense of the reality I have developed for myself? Have I gone to the point of no return and is that a bad thing, considering my feelings over the past few years. The point of no return. Great song. Music does drive thought and emotion. I wish that I could play.

So what comes next? I know where happiness lies but it comes with a hefty price. No win situations leave much to be desired. Which situation sucks most is the question I suppose. I think that this is the place that I am in. Time to use time to think and verbalize and to be truly honest, especially to myself.

I suppose there has always been warnings or tell tale signs of a problem. There has always been anxiousness about the future. I have always preoccupied myself with what was to be and how it would come about and what it might look like. There has always been an uneasiness about being completely happy and devoid of the what if scenarios. That explains marriage numbers one through two. We are now speaking of the impending end of number three. I suppose it is what has locked me into my former current situation, as now I live in a box. The box, my hovel, though is getting more comfortable and more reliable.

Happiness has been something that has been elusive and flirtatious. Flirting has offered the happiness that I have been looking for and starving for all these years. Another nice segues. It's interesting how life offers new options every now and then. For the first time, there is a connection with someone that is truly deep, meaningful, sensual, and sexual and fulfilling, one that brings a smile to my face that borders on ridiculous. Thinking of it reminds me of the Joker on the Batman television series.

Chemistry was never a welcome topic in school for me. I endured it during oceanography and marine bio classes in high school because it was hands on. You actually did stuff in school that wasn't just out of a textbook, like calculus or algebra. Chemistry now is the be all and end all.

The reactions that we have for one another is intoxicating to the point of being in our own world as the world around us spins miserably out of control. Within our axis there is peace and tranquility. Chemical reactions often involve smell, an incredibly powerful toxin. Certain smells will trigger reactions of absolute joy and heartfelt warmth. The smell of hair conditioner, if just the right one enjoys a reaction like no other. While I am clueless to the symbols on the periodic chart, I am well aware of the chemistry between two people when the chemistry gels.

Socrates said, "Know thyself." Two words that emerge as powerful metaphors for the meaning of life, for the very existence of ones own soul. One needs to come to terms with who they are, how they got there and where are they heading. By coming to terms with who you are, individuals should be able to take advantage of opportunities as they present themselves. For some it takes more than knowing yourself, it takes courage and inner strength to make changes for the better. Knowing yourself will give you insight as to how you may handle the negative ramifications of using your courage and inner strength. In essence, it becomes a determination of how you want to live your life and is manifested in day-to-day existence as anticipated outcomes. I think I am tired, because I haven't clearly conceptualized in my mind what meaning should be associated with this paragraph. My hovel is feeling a little more comfortable. It is like living in a college dormitory without the socialization. There is something to be said for peace and quiet with only your own mind to create the sounds. It isn't always a good thing; I certainly would not have thought so months ago.

As it happens, this morning I had some ideas flow through. Perhaps tomorrow morning will bring the same fortune. Good night.

I did have a couple of ideas run through my mind this morning as I ran through the streets. Some of it had to do with age and sincerely throwing around the idea of a long term and life altering change. Life altering in the sense that perhaps happiness would be around the corner. I am concerned about that though. Is depression a life long event that manifests itself when a turbulent event arises or is it induced specifically by an event and then lingers for a time until the crisis has past? That being said, should the happiness that I envision just ahead be compromised by depression and mood swings that may bring a repeat of events or will that be able to kept in check by first the genius of medical research and secondly by an even greater event, true expression of fulfillment? Sounds great on paper, but really, who the fuck really knows.

To you my reader, whomever you may be, this writing probably comes across as quite self-centered. But I have given myself the liberty of writing in such a way in order to put my thoughts in order. I am writing this for my own clarity and sanity as well as satisfaction and not for your amusement or for you to sit in judgment. Only I am capable of judging and punishing myself, as I deem necessary, hence, the box. You know that was quite sanctimonious. The box is a temporary and affordable abode.

It snowed today. As usual you can count on the weather folks to make much ado about nothing. If it weren't for Shakespeare, who would have come up with that phrase? Actually, I wonder if he originated it in the first place. Even caring whether he did or didn't is much ado about nothing. It is quiet here tonight, as it has been on every other night in my new residence. I spent some time doing something that keeps me focused and centered, my job on Wall Street. I like to work on my craft by reading and using pieces that I have gathered from teaching a course in financing in one of the colleges of New York City. I suppose if I raise my own standards, then those around me will be forced to raise theirs and like a domino negotiating it's way around itself, success will be found when the last domino falls.

The morning after a snowfall is typically pretty. The sun is shining brightly and there is no wind to speak of. It is quiet outside; there is no movement save the rare car and infrequent rumblings of the Long Island Railroad. Small ghostlike shrouds of snow trail aimlessly chasing emptiness after the last car of the rolling cars pass by. Wisps of snow chase aimlessly after the train almost as if grasping at a last chance. A new morning can be viewed as more of the same or yet another opportunity for a new beginning. I suppose it is the action of making a choice to see what the day brings forth.

I find the snow to be relaxing and romantic. The snow is a means to find a great escape. The imagination runs wild on a day as pretty as this. Possibilities come to the forefront of the mind. Days like this with the sun shining brightly and the snow a comfortable blanket on the landscape are made for finding the time to take a drive to someplace new and walk aimlessly in the quiet.

Does anyone have a perfect relationship? That is a ridiculous question. Why do people stay together these days anyway? Sense of family, sense of belonging, sense of urgency. How many people are happy in that situation? How many people are afraid of doing anything about it? I have always been afraid of doing something. Now I have done enough to force her hand because I couldn't say those elusive three words again and that I need to have some time and some space alone. I am feeling very flat at the moment. I just turned on the Sopranos for the first time because I have HBO in my box. What are they talking about? The husband having an affair. I wonder if Ozzie did anyone besides Harriet? It can't just be the times can it? Hmmm. Something to ponder for a while.

What does the term gut feeling really mean? Someone asks you for your gut feeling; what do you think is going to happen? How do you think you are going to feel in a month? Who the hell knows? I am working on day to day and handling the feelings that I have in that way. I don't think that I miss being home. Solitude is good for the soul, at least I hope that it is. I have worked out the financials and I can handle this for a while. I know that if I go back I have to make a lifelong commitment and renew vows that I don't believe in right now, especially this being the third strike. The third attempt at marriage. I am watching Sex in the City for the first time this evening. The main character needs more time before committing to marriage and the man wants to know if things will be different 3 months from now, 6 months from now, etc. It sounds like my life for the past, what, forever?

I started writing this journal just a few nights ago. I wish that I had had the foresight to think of this years ago. It is very appealing to be able to have a conversation with yourself and try to put things into perspective. While the laptop doesn't talk back, it is patient enough to sit and wait, rest if it needs to until an answer is formulated. It realizes that I need some time to wrestle with the questions in a way that will make sense to me and in a way that will give me an opportunity to sit and think without having to come up with an instant seat of the pants answer that may just be a typical task avoidance question.

Sleep didn't come for a while last night and when it did it didn't last very long. I had this one thought running through my mind and I guess it was there long enough for me to want to add it here. I had read a book by Robert Heinlen probably twenty years ago. It was a great story entitled Stranger in a Strange Land. Freud would probably read into this as a manifestation of my life at the moment. Although not a big fan of this icon, who am I to argue with his opinion, regardless of the fact that I have adopted it as my own at the moment. If I recall correctly, the story dealt with identities and identifying yourself in a larger setting. It was a long time ago but the book obviously left an impression. Books often do that. I think that the best book I had ever read was Ayn Rand's The Fountainhead. I remember the character vividly. Howard Rourke, an architect whom regardless of the outcome of events that he created or was effected by, stood by his principles. She was a literary genius who developed characters and plot so realistically that you easily find yourself immersed in the characters dilemma and life from beginning to end. I became a big fan of her writing reading everything she wrote. I later became a great fan of Hemingway reading at least a half dozen or so of his books. He too had a wonderful way of bringing characters and situations to a reality so believable that you could escape from your own reality for a time. Like phases in life, I believe people must go through phases in musical and literary genre, absorbing each and then moving on to learn more.

I suppose this is why writers write in the first place, to escape from their reality and create one that they can escape to. Making money is probably up on the list as well. Good writing is as magical as a piece of jazz, a still life black and white photograph or a piece of modern dance. Each has its own reality; its own escapism and each create a life beyond itself. It is as if they each have their own fate and destiny and capture its audience, if they are willing, to come along for the sojourn.

A rainy beginning of the day gently moved to sunshine as the last of the clouds continued to break up and drift away from the island. The sight of the sun acts as a reminder that there is ongoing renewal and potential to all whom will allow it. The sun and the clouds are linked with one another for all eternity. Clouds will not exist without the sun. It is a dependent to the sun, but the sun may not be able to be seen should the clouds protest too much. They do not form a symbiotic relationship the way certain fish swim with sharks to clean the food off them and in return are protected. Nonetheless, their relationship is strong and without question. It is a measurement that has no equal. You might say that their course runs parallel to that of the human condition, specifically the relationship between man and women. Moods change as often as the wind blows. Surprises emerge from time to time as quickly as the clouds part to let in the sun for the renewal. Clouds may return from time to time and linger about for what may seem and eternity until a break emerges. So goes the life cycle of human relationships. It is the routines and patterns that emerge that become comforting, no rather expected. Comforting relates to something completely different than this metaphor. Comforting would be the patterns and routines that are expected and desired. Comforting like the image of sitting wrapped in a blanket sipping wine in front of a roaring fireplace with light sensual jazz faintly heard in the background.

Forceful and contrived words. Forceful and contrived can also be seen as a metaphor for relationships that have faltered and lost their way.

So what did Hemingway, Updike, or Philip Roth and other literary giants do when the words wouldn't come? I wonder about the musical giants in jazz. What did Coltrane, Miles Davis, Charlie Parker and dozens of others do when the music didn't gel? Dissonance. Musical genius for making notes under normal conditions that don't blend, actually blend and produce incredible music. Quite inspirational as a matter of fact. Jazz. I have started listening to some of the jazz music that I often listened to as a kid years ago. I have found that I watch television much less than I have in the past and use it mainly as background noise while I work. Much of the time that I spend in my new abode, the laptop is on and is used as my stereo. The Internet can get me any music that I want to hear at any time I want it. Right now I am listening to a twenty minute bass solo by legendary bassist, Stanley Clark. Following this song are a dozen or so John McLaughlin pieces, Chick Corea pieces, which are then in turn followed by Charlie Parker. If this doesn't inspire you to do anything you may put your mind to, check your pulse.

Jazz is to music as free thought writing is to literature. Rock music, pop music and the like are all form fitted and must follow a structure. Jazz reinvents itself as it goes along. Jazz musicians take you on a journey through their imagination, through their soul and through their very being. There are no rules, no parameters, no guidelines, just a free flowing of expression and passion. Jazz takes you through changing moods, changing colors, changing seasons and changing affects. It can do this in one song, on one album or any combination. It can leave you breathless and frightened or in awe. It can leave you focused enough to climb the tallest obstacle or saddened and pained in a valley of despair. Remarkably, it can do this without words. Remarkably too, I would imagine that each composition leaves its listeners with different visions and different scars that are brought back to life or times of great joy, happiness and bright, vibrant colors. Arguably, you might be able to say that music is a catalyst for personal introspection because it sets the mood and more than likely, creates the mood for you to take the time to investigate yourself. Case in point, I didn't start expressing through the keyboard on my laptop until the music began. Thank you Al Dimeola and John McLaughlin for setting the stage.

Hope is a fundamentally empowering word. It is universal and cares not for the barriers of language, culture or religion. Equally, it has no patience for demographics and socioeconomic status. It knows no boundaries and knows no obstacles except for those artificially placed on it by the one holding out for hope. Hope needs to be acted upon and perhaps needs faith. I am the last one that you would want to have a discussion of religion with, but I do see that people need something to believe in. My contention is that the faith and belief that one has is one that is created by the holder of hope. It is my personal philosophy that you have to show me something tangible and provide credible and irrefutable evidence of some greater being. Otherwise, the writers of the Judeo-Christian bibles or writers of the Koran are on par with the literary genius' that have withstood the test of time. Personal faith and belief in oneself and what one can do and what one needs to do in order to change their life is strictly in their control. The faith is personal and powerful if acted upon. One need not pray to an invisible god and ask for salvation or ask for pity or guidance. Who is answering you if not your reflective self? Things happen for a reason, don't they? That is what fate is. Is there some kind of predestination for everyone or is there a reason that things happen? I suppose on some level that I believe in fate. Fate isn't an organized religion that preaches consequences however. Is fate what you make of it or do you create fate as you negotiate through life? I have always found these to be interesting questions that have no reliable and hard and true answer. Belief is a very personal aspect of the human condition. Because we are a freethinking species, what we chose to do with these views, in most cases is our choice.

I am thinking that perhaps I need to change the name of this document. It is currently listed as hovel. It isn't a hovel any longer. It is comfortable and quiet. On certain levels it parallels Henry David Thoreau's journey to the woods at Walden Pond. Excuse me for a minute as I turn back to my music list and scroll through the pieces that I have downloaded and see if there may be any appropriate names for my document, or for that matter, my abode. It comes down to two possibilities. First is Crazeolgy by Miles Davis and John Coltrane or secondly, Phase Dance by Pat Metheny. I think for the time being anyway, Phase Dance gets the nod.

I thought that would have been easy. Now I have to read into the choice that I made and try to figure out how my meaning will be interpreted. I don't know who will be reading this if anyone, but nonetheless, I have created some type of wedge. Phase Dance; clearly chosen because of its readily apparent meaning to you. Readily apparent I think anyway. Am I in the middle of a phase of life and moving through it like a dancer? If so, the dancer is clumsy and awkward. I did mention that I was not phased by the situation as if nothing has happened of any consequence. Therefore, this title is gone. Crazeology. Can't get any clearer or vivid than that can it? Am I crazy for what I am doing? I think not. I am in control of my fate, my destiny or predestination, however you choose to view its complexities. All right, both names are history. How about something as simple as the town I am in? Not nearly as powerful or eloquent as Walden.

New title. 6112. 6112 is the number of the post office box that I opened last week. It is my new mailing address. It will be more permanent than my temporary living arrangements and is as small as my current accommodations. It is simple. It is powerful yet not overbearing. It is not eloquent but it gives my story meaning and a sense of belonging. It leaves me comfortable. I don't see any mental haggling over this simple, yet revealing title. Nothing that I would have to analyze for misconstrued meaning. It is at once comforting and telling as well as satisfying.

It is martini time and Pat Metheny time. The two together usually produce thoughts and images and relative truths. I feel somewhat isolated but not alone. I have had that feeling all day today; no reason, just have. That would be typical. It is very quiet here tonight. Just the two of us; my thoughts and myself. All at once I am not sure where I am going with this entry this evening. I am entertaining the thought of completely relaxing in the solitude. But as usual, that is never an easy task for me. I am always on; always thinking, always have to analyze. But I don't want to do that tonight. I was just want to go with the flow, just ease into the evening and enjoy it. Time for another martini.

Let's talk about obsessions for a moment. Is the job as a Wall Street banker my obsession or was it a professional goal? Wasn't it really the idea that it would mean that I was really somebody? Was it something that I had to prove to myself or prove to others? In fact it was probably the others who I haven't seen in a lifetime and probably wouldn't anyway. I definitely know that I wanted to be someone before my high school reunion. It's funny; I became a partner in the firm before my twenty-year reunion. I didn't go. Ironic.

I have held it pretty much together for my entire life. At some point the tightrope has to unravel leaving the walker in an untenable position. For an instant that tightrope walker has to face his or her demons and make peace with their inner self and soul. It is at that point that one faces their inevitable breakdown. Securing a safety net is the only preventative medicine. The sheer terror lasts for a fleeting moment, at which point the walker must face the reality of his or her situation and make decisions that will impact not only the walker, but also the cast of characters that surround him or her.

In my case, anti-depressants have been my safety net for the past several months. Without it, the tightrope walker would fall from greater heights each time until the net below could no longer handle the impact of the relentless pounding. I know longer feel myself fighting myself or going ten rounds with my depression. I feel myself feeling more and more relaxed and more like the person I once knew. It is as if I am rereading a novel that I haven't seen in some time. I am reacquainting myself with the lead character and once again familiarizing myself with the nuances that were once a great part of the entire landscape.

It is a gentle movement, like the flickering dance of a candle illuminating a darkened room. A single entity carrying enormous power and fortitude. Small, fragile looking flicker standing only 2—3 centimeters high. Let the fool who underestimates this tiny urchin get burned but once and all at once its height grows with new perspective. Let not the fool misinterpret the singular meaning of the flame. Passion, heat, virility, strength, warmth, caring and understanding. It signifies a new beginning, a destiny and fate not yet reached.

Let us not forget that the flame too will engulf you and extinguish the air around you suffocating the very life you seek from you. The flame also stands as a reminder to pain and suffering if you allow it too. I see it though as a measure of ones love for another person. The flame asks for nothing in return save the match to keep it burning bright for an eternity. And on that metaphor, I bid you a good night.

It has been a few nights since I have last entertained the thought of writing. There is, in my mind anyway, a very fine line that delineates that which is fantasy and that which is reality. I imagine that I have spent a great deal of time on the fantasy side of the field. Probably a bit more than I would like to admit. I think that I truly realized that last night, although now I would say that the feeling of dread as dissipated to a great extent. Nothing seems, as it should until you are sitting face to face with your past, present and future all at the very same time. That was last night sitting in the therapist's office as our weekly triad. The number three. The third wife. The three in conversation.

This relationship too unraveled and was left lying naked and vulnerable to scrutiny and questions. It left me naked and vulnerable and questioning my own behavior and mindset. I keep coming up with the same question; will I ever be happy? I am afraid of the answer that I keep coming up with. Regardless of the outcome of this domestic situation, will I be any use or any good to anyone? For a fleeting moment on the drive home tonight, I thought of a tree. That is never a good sign especially on a motorcycle. I guess I will have to keep a closer eye on myself. What the hell does that mean? I'm done for now. There isn't going to be anything profound to write this evening.

Ryan took a break and put the manuscript down. He was mentally and physically exhausted. He poured himself another glass of bourbon. It dawned upon him that he was reading what amounted to a suicide note. He didn't even know if John meant it to be one or if he had hoped he would have read it sooner. This was obviously his way of asking for help and Ryan wasn't there for him. Tears began to stream down his face as he polished off the glass with one long gulp and poured another. The dogs hadn't stirred. The house was quiet. He continued to read.

It is like being in a science fiction novel. It doesn't really matter by whom it is written because when you get down to it they pretty much follow the same typical format. In my scenario or scenarios, I am in the middle of a temporal space shift where the main character can move from one dimension to the other. The main character is in a holding pattern, not knowing in which dimension to rest, because the two dimensions exclude one another. There is a sense of pull to each of the parallel dimensions. Imagine if you would, a simple instructional tool used to teach children about similarities and differences. The Venn Diagram with it's three rings. The characters two-dimensional life with the character firmly entrenched in the center ring.

The thought of the center ring brings the circus to mind. While I do not portray my life at the moment as a circus, I do feel as if the audience is waiting for the next act of the performance. Just like an author toying with its readers or a puppeteer pulling the strings of its puppet, the readers are getting restless for movement. There has to be a direction taken and a stand made. At the moment, however, I am not ready to write the conclusion of this tale, although I feel that to some degree the ending has been preordained.

"Holy shit."

The room felt smaller today; somewhat confining and claustrophobic. Riding my motorcycle is always good at times like this, especially when there is bright sunshine and blue skies. It was a good ride. I felt better for a time, almost to the point where, dare I say it, relaxing. But all it takes is a moment to change all of that. I have felt a regression of sorts for the past several days. I have that feeling again of being lost and confused and without direction. I have been very focused at work, planning various things including acquisitions, mergers and maybe just a little stock manipulation. It helps me to keep busy and then as a result I don't have to think about life and the obstacles that stand before me or the obstacles that I place before me.

Over the last day or two I have felt the darkness slowly creeping back into my life. I simply don't find things funny as I have over the past several weeks. It is as if a gray cloud has cast a shadow over me and the sun has been replaced by rain. I felt very unfocused at work today. The file on my desk went untouched as task avoidance strategies took hold. I still have several days in which to complete the work in the file. It isn't even as if it were difficult or even really time consuming. I just cannot seem to motivate myself to complete, although complete it I must and I know that I will. Maybe I will look at it tonight after I complete this entry. It isn't as if I am writing anything new tonight. It isn't as if I am writing anything of any value or profound and deep explorations of the mind and soul. I'm not quite sure that I have done that in any of the previous pages either.

The Olympics are about to come on. There is so much energy, so much promise and potential for individuals to grow and to make something out of an opportunity. These young men and women have their whole lives in front of them to make choices, both wrong and right and to do something special with their lives. They have a chance to leave a legacy. That's funny. Not many people know their legacy. I suppose you can imagine what your legacy would be after your passing.

So when does drinking do something positive for you? I mean aside from putting on another face, what positives come out of going beyond drinking socially? Drinking socially is the one, perhaps a second martini, but not one beyond that. Well, this is my 6th glass of wine. The question beckons; am I happy yet now that I have completely loosened up? No. To make matters worse, it is raining now and probably will tomorrow morning as well. Rain never does anything positive for my mood. Being alone doesn't do anything for it either. This place is so small…how small is it? It is so small that I can work on the laptop, touch the television, take something out of the refrigerator and put my feet up on the bed all at once. Maybe I will feel better when I have a bigger place. I hope so!!! God I hope so!! Sorry can't use god. Don't quite believe in the existence of the invisible all-powerful omnipotent do all and be all-spiritual being. My medicine man wanted to know whom I was writing for? I said for no one. He asked if the writing was helping me to clarify things? I answered no to that one also.

Ryan felt that his friend John was reaching the breaking point. He had hidden it so well, though. Who would have thought this? What if he had read this when John gave it to him? Would it have changed anything?

Mood swings are interesting. Words like resiliency, perseverance, courage and sacrifice immediately come to mind. I feel much better now, somewhat uplifted and I have no reason for the change. Maybe it is that time of the month. Could you imagine if men had their periods too? I hope this doesn't come off too sexist, but what a fucking world it would be if everyone and their mother, (father too) were ovulating at the same time. There wouldn't be any wars. There would be huge cable subscriptions to the Lifetime channel, though. Men would actually read what was on Oprah's got to read list. Poignant and poetic.

I wonder if I am allowed to smoke in here. I feel like having a cigar. I suppose I can just blow it out of the window. I suppose the room would smell of cigar smoke. The whole fucking place smells like smoke, so who would know the fucking difference? I can be smarter than everyone else here. I am going to turn my window fan inside out and blow the air right the fuck out of here. Okay, I have started on the cigar, which sucks by the way. The fan idea was shear brilliance. Almost time for the air freshener spray. Note to others: as I have done, please make sure that you cover your martini when spraying the air freshener. One must never tinker with the dynamics and ambiance of the martini.

The worst part of a cigar is the aftertaste. It probably can be compared to sucking on the tailpipe of an eighteen-wheel tractor-trailer. This room could probably use a black light poster. I gave myself a chuckle with that retort. I can use a chuckle. This is so fucking pathetic. It is a good thing that I don't smoke pot. That would be the next indulgence.

I don't know where this is all coming from tonight. It is as if there is combinations of I don't give a shit what anyone thinks or says or infers along with sliding down the path towards depression and feeling sorry for myself, which is very unbecoming. (I used shit instead of fuck this time just to change up the lousy vocabulary). I am pretty sure that I am not manic depressant, but this mood change is ridiculous. I might as well strap on a tampon. That reminds me. That is exactly what I looked like today skiing. I had a red ski bib on and a red Lands End winter jacket. Just call me Bloody Mary.

This is probably why they say not to drink while on anti-depressants. What am I supposed to do? I am past the driving into the embankment phase. Drinking is evil. If I were Christian, I guess at this point I would begin to think about being a born again Christian and saving the world. But then I wound sound like George Bush and lose all credibility. The details would reflect of course that I can't even save myself. Maybe alcohol poisoning. Now I am getting stupid. I am going to lay down for a while and see if anything intelligent comes to mind. Not likely, though.

Ryan poured himself another bourbon. He stood and stretched and this caught the attention of the dogs. "Let's go dummies. Everyone outside." The dogs jumped up immediately and ran out of the back door.

I ask you; what rivals the sheer splendor and vigor of the oncoming of spring? I think that it can be argued that is unparalleled to anything else. It is quite extraordinary if you take the time to observe it. To sit back and use the powers of observation, you can make the argument that it is both subtle and extreme all at once. The nuances of early buds and the singing of birds in their infancy are intertwined with the ducks and geese that have spent their time waiting in the water as the surface ice begins to thaw all around them.

Ryan sipped some more of his bourbon. John is all over the place. He is up and down at the same time.

Spring represents all that is new and all that is beautiful. The sounds of a babbling brook that was there but went all but unnoticed during the winter, now stands out in a cacophony of sounds. Spring brings the forth the opportunity for rebirth. It is the sounds of renewal and the opportunity to start a new chapter, or even a new beginning. It was as great deal for a motorcycle ride. I put on my helmet and opened up the throttle of my black Harley.

I couldn't wait to get back here and use the inspiration of the day to have words flow through the fingertips and onto the keyboard without the use of adult beverages to stoke the fire. A variety of words, phrases and metaphors were spreading through my mind in an attempt to find just the right words, phrases and metaphors to use here. It was almost lyrical and whimsical. I had the feeling that I wanted to write song lyrics. I don't want to push it though. They have to be natural and not contrived or forced. I'll know when the time is right. I'll feel like Bette Middler or Barbara Streisand (before politics).

Half way through my ride this morning, I stopped to listen and to watch. The power of observation is one that I feel that to many people ignore. The woodpeckers were hard at work busying themselves for the spring. Geese were flying overhead in a flock of ten to twelve birds. Only two were squawking, one in the front and one responding in the rear. These two birds made communication seem quite easy. Several minutes later, two geese flying closely together made their way to their destination. The sounds and smells of the oncoming spring can do more to lift a person spiritually than can ever be imagined.

So how does one come to terms with changes in life, whether fragmented over time or a complete overturning of the mind, soul and spirit? Time can be a painful reminder of what could be, should be or what may never be. So I sit here in the dark wearing comfortable pajama bottoms bought with money when money finally became a non-issue after spending so long to reach that ability to spend without thinking too much into the actual purchase.

This was the first paragraph that I had written so many weeks ago when I began this literary venture. The answer came clearly this evening. One comes to terms with such conditions through financial statements and anticipated success. One door closes as another one opens, goes the saying.

It is said that things do happen for the best. While I still cannot fathom the enormous financial burden that befalls me now, it seems to be somewhat counterintuitive to think of the future as a simple bank statement. Last night Dana and I went to a local pub for drinks and dinner. I'm sorry, I haven't properly introduced you to Dana, have I? We laughed, we had conversation and we had kisses across the table. We looked into each other's eyes while talking about anything we wanted too. I didn't have the all too familiar feeling of having to move conversations elsewhere or have to work to find something slightly interesting to discuss. Moreover, I didn't have to eat with someone else and feel that I was dining alone because there wasn't any conversation. I met Dana while working out at the gym just a few weeks ago. Tigers don't change their stripes, do they?

Wife number one thinks that I have to get my priorities in order and my head set on straight. She goes on to say that in order to get better I have to deal with the issues. She thinks I avoid the issues. She says that I have avoided dealing with this impending third divorce. I am dealing with it; I took a tranquilizer and washed it down with a martini.

You know, for such a financial genius as I am, you would have thought that I would have learned from the first two mistakes and written up a pre-nuptial. That is love for you. It makes you blind and stupid. And poor.

While I cannot say that I have really enjoyed reading Walden, I do see his anger and contempt for society and its ills. I can't say that I agree with Thoreau's analysis, but again, it provides an interesting perspective. I typically see the good in all people and society as a whole. I am certainly not naïve. Believing that there are many people who have agendas and personal missions that may negatively impact and affect others around them is reality. I would not be accused of being cynical although I might make comments that would reflect that designation.

The one common factor that I share with Thoreau at the moment is the need for solitude and quiet and a chance to reflect. Where we differ significantly is my need to improve myself and continue to build. I need to work and work hard where I can feel that I can and will make a contribution to the society that he shuns.

Now the anti-Walden. I have felt the need, want or desire, whichever word is most appropriate, to buy something. Not just something, but rather something toy specific. I think that I would like to purchase a kayak. That's pointless. I will use it once and forget it. I think that perhaps I would like to buy a Triumph Spitfire TR6 from the 1970s. But fortunately, I haven't fed into this impulsiveness. Instead I impulsively bought a book from Amazon.com that I had read about in Newsday sometime this past week. I had even been given an opportunity by newsday.com to read excerpts from chapter one. The book is entitled A Multitude of Sins and is written by Richard Ford. There are short stories around the theme of adultery, the road towards it and consequences of it. I have an absolute fascination with the topic and obviously a vested interest on the topic as well as perspective and respect for the need to find love, compassion and happiness elsewhere. It is also a rather selfish act for which I punish myself every now and then with a bout of depression and a ready remedy of vodka.

It is a bright sunny day outside. The difference between inside and outside today is, thankfully, my mood. Outside it is extremely blustery with winds rising and falling like the ebb and flow of the tides. Inside is the calm and peacefulness of a lake at sunset.

I sometimes wonder if the nuances of inanimate objects tell the story of a reality. This evening I hooked up my laptop to optimum on line to find out that there probably isn't enough power at the line from the pole near the street to let the internet do what it does; transmit messages, whether in code or digital music from one source to another. So after spending some time with the technician on the phone, I find out that once again, a technician will be coming to me and yet again, a third again, I will have to be available for them. Somewhat annoyed that I wouldn't be on line this evening, I shut down the computer. For some undeterminable reason, the computer would not shut down. Since it runs on electricity and/or a battery backup, I chose to pull the plug and let the computer battery run the course of its electrical life. As the computer began its final breath of electrical impulses, the computer began to beep as a patient on a heart monitor beeps as he begins to gasp and realize that the end is fast approaching. As the battery wound down, the beeping became faster, almost as a prelude to a flat line. The sounds of this slow death increased in speed, until, with utter finality, there was only silence. It seemed to me to be a poignant moment. It seemed to simply be a metaphor to our banal existence, nothing more than a foreshadowing to an ever-present finality. Death! My death?

I received my book yesterday, A Multitude of Sins. I am well beyond the halfway point and have come to realize the pain and anger that I have caused. She certainly never deserved what I have put her through this last year. She is the victim of a husband who could find no happiness at home. A husband who was married to his job and needed something more from life than the current existence. At a point, it was nothing more than an existence, one that the husband could no longer endure, emotionally and spiritually, although everything material was at his fingertips. However, she did not deserve just the existence of a husband.

Melissa deserves like all men and women, to be loved completely. I could not do it and could no longer pretend to or try to invent a way to love her the way that she was meant to be loved. I couldn't even bring myself to lie and tell her that I loved her just to keep things going. It would not have been right or just for either of us. It would be the slow death of the laptop, beeping its final sounds as the last of the electrical impulses found its way across the seemingly endless passages of wires and chips. There would certainly be no benefit for either of us in the short term, much less the long term.

I have had an overwhelming urge to travel. I want to see the world in all of its glory and see the highlights of nature's splendor and devastations. It is these two worlds that are forever intertwined in each other's presentations. It is as if mankind stands on the precipice of an ongoing dawning, a new daily beginning to the unlimited and boundless beauty that Earth provides us with.

Oscar Wilde wrote, "...just as man represents the triumph of mind over morals" in his novel, The Picture of Dorian Gray, it struck me as quite interesting of how pervasive this notion is in the western culture. It is as if all men have this constant battle within themselves to rationalize their indiscretions. Man generally knows the difference between right and wrong in others and is typically quick to judge. I wonder how many men judge themselves as harshly as I have judged myself over this period. I, John Sizemore, knew the difference between right and wrong, but nonetheless played my part in this affair because I knew that I had too. I was quite aware of the consequences, but at times I don't think I understood them. There were times I think that a lack of reality played a part in this dramatic unfolding of life. Wilde went on to write, "Faithfulness is to the emotional life what consistency is to the life of the intellect—simply a confession of failure." I am not quite sure how I intend to react to this phrase, but I know that it has intrigued me. Is he talking about remaining stagnant and within the box as self-awareness of what one can be but won't attempt to rise above the present situation? If that is so, then I suppose I would tend to agree with his analysis.

After some time I moved. I call the new place the chalet. The chalet seems a bit smaller today. It's like one of those cabins that you would see in the movies. Very cozy, very quiet and peaceful. It has everything but a fireplace and a lake at the foot of the property. It was a rather uneventful day. I just wanted to be outside but not really do much of anything.

Dana and I spent several hours with a bottle of wine just sitting and having one conversation after the other. It was truly a wonderful experience. To sit and have a flow of dialog that had meaning and consequence with someone whom you are intimately involved is something worth taking the opportunity to explore. More accurately would be if I had written that I never felt comfortable until now to have an intimate conversation and a discussion of goals and dreams with someone that I am intimate with. I loved it. It was both rewarding and fulfilling. It was easy and insightful into the mind of one whom you are so involved as well as to oneself. I highly recommend such an opportunity to all.

I also highly recommend having a good cigar and fine glass of wine while reflecting and writing. It is inviting and relaxing at the same time. Good music in the background is also helpful. It has typically been jazz of one genre or another. Tonight it will be Blood, Sweat and Tears. Not a tremendous departure from jazz and blues but just as stimulating.

I was looking through some old things this morning, being a little nostalgic. Very little. I have always felt that what's behind you is behind you. I never had much for personal history. I like to look forward to what will be. Ironic though, I enjoy history. I enjoy reading about life in the past. Three of my favorite books were either written about previous life or written in a time that was current then, but just as provocative as if it were written today. The Fountainhead, The Pillars of the Earth and A Tale of Two Cities.

The calm before the storm, Ryan questioned himself.

My colleague's face is pale, drawn and he appears to be thirty to forty years older than he is in actuality. After he shakes the sleep from his listless body, he begins to tell me that he has lost all ability to maintain his position as a leader in the firm. He has lost all ability to foster a culture of reform or to maintain standards and expectations. He attributes this to the loss of the woman he loves. She apparently has left without explanation and he has desperately tried to track her down in various cities and towns. She is a foreigner and as such feels she would have trouble blending in anywhere but where he is. I made attempts to offer ways to help his troubled mind, but soon found myself quiet and forlorn. After what seemed to be several minutes of an uncomfortable solitude, I awoke from my dream. The task now is to sit back and reflect upon the dream and see what meaning I may invoke from it if any, although I am rather sure that I will be able to determine something significant from this. The emotional and the spiritual component of this dream is where I probably will derive some meaning. I do have some concern for my colleague who more than likely will not make partner again this year and my inability to offer help or council.

It is three fifteen in the morning. Sleep is that elusive animal that one hunts for but the camouflage of the forest protects the prey. I polished off another book, but that did not seem to help. I'd try warm milk if I believed that that was a viable solution. Perhaps there is something on television worth watching. Not likely as there isn't much aside from sports to keep you riveted to the box during the day. There aren't too many options from which to choose at this point. I think that there is too much thinking going on right now and that is keeping me away from sleep and then dreams.

On my way into work this morning I was struck by several familiar observations, which then moved into several flashbacks to last spring. The intricacies and power of the olfactory system can never be underestimated or unappreciated. There was a particular smell in the air this morning, I am not sure if it had to do with the increase in temperature or if it is just a natural phenomenon to this time of year. The temperature, that something quality in the air that you can't quite put your finger on along with the wrong choice of music this morning brought be back a year to a time when time itself was breathing heavily down my neck.

Pictures of driving recklessly last year were visuals that I had all the way to the parking lot this morning. The big difference is that I am quite in control these days or at least I think I am.

Another smell this morning that brought back some uneasy feelings was the smell of the office lobby this morning. It was clearly the odor of the building at this time last year. The smell of the elevator with the familiar aftershave of the managing partners. After getting involved in some work this morning, the uneasy feelings began to quell and I worked my way back into a comfortable routine.

The senses are the fabric of the human condition. They bring up feelings that have been long been suppressed as well as being an invitation to new experiences. The sense of smell is strongly linked to the basic operation of breathing. Breathing is the natural process by which we are sustained. The analogy I am trying to create here is one that links the basic necessities of life, which includes love and the love of life. For me then, cheating became a basic necessity of life. In essence, I cheated in order to breathe.

I had had a pretty good today. The journal entry tonight would have been quite upbeat if I had decided to even write this evening. I was listening to some good music; some Van Morrison and then Bon Jovi live. That is until I opened my mail. The divorce is official. Three is a charm isn't it? It is somewhat surreal and numbing at the same time. The only thing that I am thinking about is what she must be feeling or going through right now. So now I am listening to classical music and I think it is a good time for a glass of wine.

A change in the chemical interactions in the body is one way to change the personal atmosphere that one faces. Lifting weights creates a flow of certain chemicals; I believe to be endorphins that help to alter the state of mind. It helps to focus on the task at hand and serves to keep your mind occupied. Fortunately it has worked. I am listening to Don Henley's In A New York Minute, and watching a great Yankee game while paying bills electronically. I had had an urge to jump onto my bike and head for the beach, but I chose to run and work out and deal with the issues at hand. I tell you it is great to watch the Red Sox make as many infield errors as they have this evening. Maybe things are right with the world after all.

I'm pretty sure I am going to take that drive regardless. I won't be heading towards the beach, just the bank to make a quick deposit and withdrawal. I am too wound up and filled with energy to just sit here. I have had this boundless energy all day. I walked the office several times and spoke to some of my contacts to keep occupied while the market grew, made corrections, fell back and inched its way up to where it began in the morning.

It has been just about four months since I began this journey or process of self-discovery, self-loathing, self-recrimination and healing. I no longer feel the urgency or the need to continue writing. I am therefore, going to cease placing entries into this document, for now anyway. Should I choose to continue, I know that it is here and it has always been a comfort to me. Perhaps as my therapist suggests, there isn't a need to write in here and open up for no one in particular, but that I have Dana to open up to and that has replaced the journal. Sounds like a plan.

*

I feel as if I should travel somewhere by myself. I haven't taken the necessary steps to get better mentally. I am moving from one relationship to another. It doesn't feel quite right anymore. I still feel all the same feelings and needs and nothing has changed except the women. I am thinking of a permanent vacation.

Oh, fuck thought Ryan. This *is* a suicide note. He wanted me to read this and stop him.

I really like Dana. I still have the same personal issues. They have never been resolved because I haven't allowed myself the time to resolve them. I haven't allowed myself the time to step out of myself and evaluate everything. I haven't allowed myself the Walden that I desperately needed; the self-reflection that I haven't allowed for myself. At this point I feel that I will only hurt Dana in the long run if I don't allow myself to work on myself. If it sounds self-serving than so be it. I know that I have repeatedly hurt her too. Perhaps I might hurt myself as well.

Perhaps at some level or at some point I deserve a little credit for having the courage to follow through and let my heart have it's way. It doesn't lessen the impact that it has had, but nonetheless it offers perspective and possibilities and perhaps some solace.

However, it is now time to say good-bye to Dana. She deserves better.

It is a year later. I met Christine Montero today. She is a waitress at my friend Ryan's place. Actually, it is called Katie's Place. I don't think that I will be seeing much of Christine or Katie's Place much anymore. If at all....

I put the papers down on my lap. I looked at the bottle of bourbon that I had made a significant dent in and wondered when John moved from martinis to bourbon. I wasn't sure what I was expecting before I had read the piece. I still wasn't sure what I was thinking about it now. I knew that I lost a friend and I had a feeling I was going to lose myself in a bottle.

VIII

When Katie woke me up a few hours later it was 3:30 in the morning and she encouraged me to come up to bed. I shook off as best as I could the cobwebs that were embedded in my mind. I tried to quietly move the dogs off but they wanted no part of that. If I'm up, they're up. They started washing my face with their tongues, so I threw them outside for a couple of minutes, pulled the orange juice from the refrigerator and gulped some down out of the container. Katie was already on her way upstairs and therefore didn't see my kitchen indiscretion.

With the dogs back in, I made my way upstairs towards what I expected would be a restless and fitful sleep, filled with dark dreams and images hanging over me like the smog of a hot, humid Los Angeles afternoon.

A car door slams shut. The impact in itself is loud enough to make the rats at the dump scurry away in fright. He is dressed in black, as is his custom. The body is dumped without care or affect. It is simply a job to be performed. It is one of those vocations that require no W2 form or social security number. It's raining and the stench from the wasteland becomes more perverse with the addition of yet another body. He knows that these people, these perverts belong here. They deserve nothing better, but far worse. He has read Dante's Inferno and believes with all of his heart that there is a special place for these people, these plagues to society, these blots on the landscape.

He wouldn't call himself a vigilante but rather a justice of the peace. Perhaps justice for the peace would be more appropriate. More and more of these wastes of society have been allowed to prey on innocent children through the Internet. They secretly enter the world of elementary and middle school children and play on their emotions. "I'm moving into the neighborhood with my mom and dad, brother and sister. We are going to be going to your school. I'm a little nervous about it. Do you think I will fit in? It is hard to move. I am moving all the time because my mom and dad are in the army. They call me an army brat because I move from place to place. My name is Jason. What is yours?" After a few weeks the "child" moves in and wants to get together for a play date. They meet in the schoolyard and the child is never seen again.

These animals are never rehabilitated. They just become harder in prison. Instead of being the predator, they become the prey to adult sinister intentions. When they are finally released, they are angrier, more deceptive and sometimes smarter. They have no place in our community much less our world. So as Justice for Peace, I remove them from our world and put them where they so justly belong.

I have no concern of where I end up in the afterlife. My goal is the elimination of those who would prey on the young. It is my personal version of Inherit the Wind. It is survival of the fittest and these beasts are not fit for human society.

For through my justice, I have the faith that the Ninth Circle of Hell is a fitting life for the predators. They will for all eternity be placed in Cocytus, a frozen lake of ice. Like the traitors they are with, traitors to the lives of others, they will be immersed in this frozen lake with eternal tortures being performed upon them by the giants that are masters of the ninth ring. They would have their heads and shoulders above the ice with their general form curved like a crescent moon with their feet above the ice. There hands would be near their face but not near enough to protect their faces from their eternal fate.

These giants who stand 8 feet tall and have razor sharp teeth are unclothed but their form is that of a dragon with sharp scales and clubbed tail, which is used to beat these sinners repeatedly in the head. Their teeth and claws are used to gnaw the hands, fingers, feet and toes over and over.

Each sinner is allowed to painfully heal before once again being clubbed and torn apart by his or her evil spirit, colored in the red of flowing blood.

I trailed the predator from his car as he looked for his next victim's home. It was dark outside and the street he was on was dark and quiet. The trees blocked much of the moonlight and the singing of the grasshoppers and June bugs kept the sounds of crunching leaves and twigs from being overheard.

After taking his walk, the third such walk this week, in order to embed himself into the fabric of the community, he retreated to his car and returned to his small motel room. It was here where the sinner found his timely death in as vicious and painful a way imaginable. I slipped behind the newest member of the Ninth Circle Club and swung my blade with as much force as I could muster. Blood sprayed outwardly in a pattern of over 200 degrees. The forensics people would have a better number after they reviewed their protractors. The police in these matters haven't put in as much commitment into finding me as others might have hoped. Victims' families made me their champion creating websites and taking out advertisements in various magazines.

The smell of blood and waste was slowly dissipating as the new smell of fresh ground coffee began permeating the room. I slowly stretched and realized where I was and more importantly, who I was. The dream was gone, but there was a headache the size of Mount Rushmore. Katie came up with a tray of coffee and muffins and placed them on the bed. She sat down and took a cup for herself. "When you started slicing and punching in the air I knew it was time to wake you up."

"Thanks. What a dream. I was killing people and sending them to hell."

"Anyone we know?" she smiled. She sipped her coffee and then placed it down on the tray. "You look like shit", she stated.

"Thanks. Love you, too". I had a little too much to drink last night. I read something that John had written and gave me a few weeks ago. I wish that I had read it then. I might have been able to do something...I don't know...talk him out of it. Shit!"

"You don't know what was going through his mind. People just sometimes snap. They can't handle the pressure. They want to make everything go away."

"I know what was going through his mind. It was pretty dark. He was pretty descriptive in what he wrote."

"What was it poetry?"

"No. It was narrative. It was rambling, sometimes. And sometimes it was coherent. He was talking to himself most of the time. Other times he was writing as if this was a book that he wanted published. I tell you there was a lot of stuff in there. Very enlightening though. Its like someone opening their soul to be reviewed." He took a bite of a chocolate muffin and followed it up with coffee. He was starting to feel more awake. He grabbed for the container of Tylenol that he kept in his nightstand. He popped two in his mouth and chased it with the coffee. He felt the caffeine working through his veins and the muffin silencing the growl from his stomach.

"Christine is coming over later. She needs a little help getting through this. The funeral is tomorrow at 10:00."

"She say what the police came up with?"

"No foul play or anything. She said that the detectives said that the CD in the car was a Don Henley CD and that it was playing New York Minute when he turned the car off."

"Yeah, so?"

"She said the lyrics were about going away and never coming back. A guy on Wall Street who kills himself on the train tracks. Pretty creepy, don't you think?"

"Not really. I read something last night that John had written and gave me a few weeks ago. He mentions listening to that song. He mentions going on a permanent vacation. There were a lot of signs leading up to this. Nobody saw it."

"Jesus, Ryan. No wonder that you had such a bad dream. What else was in there?"

"Too much to go into. Let's just say if I read it when he gave it to me…well."

"You can't blame yourself for John's actions. That's just not fair. You can't be held responsible for the actions of other people even when you know it. Free will. Was there anything about Edgar Allen Poe in what he wrote?"

"I don't remember. Why?"

"There was a poem in his hand—Edgar Allan Poe; Dream within a Dream. It talked about days being a dream, losing hope. What else? Oh yeah—the roar of the surf and tormenting the shore and grains of sand and losing your grip."

"He was certainly sending out lots of messages. But there was no one to listen because no one knew enough to listen."

He put his coffee cup down on the tray and lay down and closed his eyes.

The sun reached across the sky and cast shadows on the bed. It was going to be another warm day, but fortunately no humidity. "Have the dogs eaten?"

"Uh huh."

"I think I'm going to grab a shower and then take them for a walk. I need to clear my head. I need to think about the menu, not these guys dressed in black in my dreams or these dark poems and stories. It's pretty fucking depressing".

He got up and headed off to the bathroom. She waited for a few minutes after the water had started. The door was ajar so she figured he didn't need or want complete privacy. She stood up and took off her shirt and shorts and headed for the bathroom. She saw through the glass doors that his head was resting on the wall and his eyes were closed. She stepped in under the running water and encircled him with her arms. He breathed a heavy sigh and began to relax. She felt him relax under her pressure. "John and I were a lot more in common that you really know. We both have this thing for music and books. Dark things too."

"Right now none of that matters. What matters is that you are here with me, right now. We have each other and that will bring us through anything."

They turned towards one another and began to kiss. They washed each other gently, washing one another's hair. There hands moved freely over each other's body. The sensations were wonderful. They both stepped out of the shower and moved back into the bedroom where they fell into each other's arms and made love. The dogs looked up and knew they weren't going to be walking anywhere anytime soon. They sighed a deep breath, one after the other and fell back asleep.

His dreams are very different this time. He thinks that making love is what life is all about. It isn't nearly about the sensation, or the act itself, but rather being entangled in one another, before, during and after. And during this entanglement being able to laugh and play with one another in a non-sexual manner as well as in a sexual manner. It is about being able to hold on as tightly as possible and get as close as possible without crushing each other. As close, physically and emotionally as we get, I can't seem to make it close enough. It is a remarkable feeling. When she falls asleep, he can just lie next to her, watch her and kiss her on her shoulders or on the back of her neck. When she awakens, he starts kissing her on her tender lips, eyes, nose and forehead the sensations come quickly back. When she stands to go to the bathroom or to get dressed or reach across for another glass of wine, he will just reach right across with her and let his lips travel throughout the length of her back to soft, supple buttocks and back up again. And just like that, any and all concerns are in the background. And as the song says, one and one doesn't equal two, one and one equals one.

She is sleeping on her side. He is cuddled up behind her. He is happy but senses something else. He hasn't figured it out but he is concerned about a growing darkness. He couldn't bring it up to Katie yet, but there was something on the fringes of his memory that seemed familiar to him. It was nothing that he could quite put his finger on, but it was there. It was on the periphery waiting to show itself. It was dark; he knew that. Whatever it was, it lay there like a thick fog on an embankment waiting for a car to make the attempt to drive through it, mistaking the edge of the road for the road; the end of the world for a continuation of the journey. It wasn't at the elusive stage yet. It hadn't landed on the tip of his tongue yet. There was nothing to put together, nothing to piece together to give her any credible evidence; the necessary picture to help with his own inner puzzle.

When he did finally realize it, it would be too late.

* * *

The ocean was quiet. The fisherman who arrived daily at 5:00 to fish were already gone and off to their day jobs. That left us alone trying to make sense of the last few days. John' s funeral was a small private affair.

Today was Monday, and the restaurant was closed. We planned on a lazy day here at our beach. Friends would be joining us later to barbeque and put down a few beers. Katie and I played Frisbee with the dogs. That didn't last long because of the types of dogs that they were. Fetch really wasn't part of their vocabulary. One would just run away with it and the other two take chase and try to take it away from him. They stood just at the water line as Katie and I took a quick swim to cool off. They barked or cried at the water, not courageous enough to take that step into the water, but knew enough that it was the water itself that kept them separated from us. We were happy.

We have always been happy. I felt the dark cloud emerge from behind the white wisps of clouds begin to form in my mind. I wasn't sure what it was, but I was certain it was bound to find me and to reveal itself to me sooner than later.

PART II

Music, when soft voices die,
Vibrates in the memory—
Odors, when sweet violets sicken,
Live within the sense they quicken.
Rose leaves, when the rose is dead,
Are heaped for the beloved's bed;
And so thy thoughts, when thou art gone,
Love itself shall slumber on.

Percy Bysshe Shelley

IX

Sheila remembers counting down from ten as the anesthetist placed the nose and mouthpiece over her face. She doesn't remember much before that except that the doctor was going to give her a sedative to relax her. The liquid moved quickly from the intravenous point to her blood stream where it traveled to her brain via arteries and veins. She felt at peace although she was being wheeled into an operating room for major heart surgery after many weeks of undergoing chemotherapy from a rapidly advancing cancer.

She was down to five when dreams and images began taking over the movie screen that was her mind. It appeared to be a lucid dream, where she knew she was dreaming and was able to alter the events as they past by in the forebrain. She dreamt of lines; circular lines, symmetric and parallel lines. She thought of lines that marked the beginning of things and marked the end of things. She dreamt of concentric circles, never ending circuitous routes that meant nothing while others led to an ending in the fashion of a labyrinth.

She controlled her images although she couldn't move past the lines. Other images appeared as metaphors, or what she thought could be metaphors. She wasn't interested in finding out what they represented, she seemed to be enjoying the free thought artwork that moved across her mind's eye. She remembered the first car that she ever rode in as a child. It was the family's first automobile. It was black and had curves that have not been captured again since the 1950's. The chrome over the wheel wells as well as the front grill had lines that were more form than function. There was a sense of architecture in each vehicle produced during this time period.

From the contour of her father's car she thought of the lines and contours of beautiful women that she had seen in movies, in print and in person. Images of Marilyn Monroe; the curves of her hips and lips; the line of her hem as it floated like wind swept clouds in the all too familiar picture of her dress playfully moving up as air was swept up from below her.

From Marilyn's wind swept dress, her inner movie screen showed wisps of steam and pan heat float upwards into a vent above the stove in her steel grey kitchen. She dreamt of the circular lines of a stemmed wine glass, filled half way with Chardonnay. The yellowish tint of the wine creating its own image in the glass as circle upon circle was established in crystal.

Her dreams slowly transformed from free flowing thought to more of a contrived, pre-established format. She remembered going to hockey games with her husband and noting the lines of the hockey stick and how the curve of the blade enabled the circular brick to fly through the air leaving an imaginary line of vapor trailing behind it as it made its way towards the piping of the goal net.

She began to think that there had to be a reason or purpose to the images she had weaved over the past…what…. how long has she been out under anesthesia? Was it minutes, hours? Could she possibly have finished with the surgery and be back in recovery? Not likely. There would be pain, there would be voices, sounds of machinery, the sound of her heart beating. Did these images serve a purpose or was she too much of an existentialist and was looking to create meaning in a vacuum?

She kept seeing one image now, over and over. It was a Native American symbol of choice. It was a labyrinth. It was a simple maze that circled in on each other. At the top was a symbol of a man. A lone figure that stood at the periphery of the labyrinth.

She had seen it in a journal recently while sitting in her doctor's office. The circle started in the center and built itself up in size as it circled itself. It seemed to take on a spirit of its very own. Was this the end of her dream? Was it the end of the long journey that was life itself? The elusive figure on the topic of the circular path—was that god? Was she heading towards the end of her self and meeting up with the second dimension of her being. Would she be an angel able to float down and silently help others, steering them out of a dangerous world and into a life of happiness? There had to be something more. This is what she was taught to believe as a child when she and her two brothers, mother and father would go to church each and every Sunday.

She felt herself getting tense. This shouldn't be happening, she wasn't ready to make a commitment to the circular path with the figure awaiting her on the top. She wanted more time with her children and grandchildren. This wasn't supposed to be the way it was going to end. The circles and line segments, the contours that she was watching in her mind were disappearing, save the one continuous white line that she saw against a backdrop of black. She new what this represented. This wasn't contrived. This wasn't free flowing thought. This was finality. This was being placed there by something outside of herself. It was a warning. No, it was an invitation to a new realm. The sound associated with this line was an alarm. But no sooner did she hear the alarm, did it disappear along with the black screen and white line.

She saw blue now. It was hazy, unfocused, and yet serene. She wasn't nervous. She was restful. A weight that she hadn't recognized throughout her life was losing its solid feeling and growing lighter. It was as if it she was buoyant. It was the hardships she had faced as an adolescent, as a young adult and finally a grown woman, hiding her face behind a veil. A veil not of deceit, but of necessity. The necessity of growing up and being responsible.

She believed she was floating on the ocean. A vast ocean of aquamarine light emanating from below the surface rather than from above. She found this odd, but didn't place much of an emphasis on determining its meaning. She floated gently in a calm current surrounded by white sand. Although she was at sea, she was surrounded as if she were in a lake. She was trying to conjure up appropriate images that would help her to distinguish what she was looking at, but realized it wouldn't serve her any good. It didn't matter at this point. She was where she was. There was no going back. She was timeless and seamless—point and lines, imaginary and visceral—but that too held no value or concern.

What mattered was what was gleaming on the surface of the bright sands—beach glass. Green, black, brown. She has seen those her entire life living off the coast of Oregon. She wanted to see what she had always searched for but never found—those elusive strains of glass—red and blue. They sat highlighted by the grains of sand for her to grasp. She reached out, her hand and arm dripping water as her appendage left the water and was able reach across time and space…she felt its aura. She was close. She was almost touching it. She could almost taste and smell it. It was within her grasp. Then she heard it…

"Time of death"…the doctor looked up at the clock at the far end of the operating room and as he slid the mask off his face, stated as a matter of fact, "16:42." She couldn't cry, as that would be the function of someone still corporeal. She felt disappointed. And then she felt…nothing.

X

The snow began to drip off the liters and gutters as he sat in the enclosed porch of their four bedroom split ranch. The winter was heading for a fall—the droplets thick with weight creating their own symphony in an off rhythm tempo. Across the street a flag is fluttering in the breeze, a mix of warm and cool air that can't seem to make up its young mind yet. Shall we continue to be winter or shall we enter the realm of yellow tulips, the violets and new colorful sprouts mixed with the early tree buds of spring? As it turned out, the weather wouldn't make up its mind for a few more days.

And it really wasn't a concern of his. He wasn't in any particular rush to be anywhere, much less leave the house. His life came to a standstill on the day the doctor told him that his wife of thirty-six years had passed away during the surgery. A moment passed before he thought enough to ask a question. "I'm sorry doctor. Her name is Sheila Talbotson—she is only 59 years old. Do you have the right patient"?

"Yes, Mr. Talbotson, I am very sorry, but it was Sheila. I am very sorry for your loss." The doctor motioned over to a nearby chair and helped Mr. Talbotson to a seat. He looked around until he found a nurse. "Nurse. Please get Mr. Talbotson here a glass of orange juice. Thanks." The nurse walked away with an acknowledgement of understanding.

"What happened? You said this would be a relatively easy surgery."

"Mr. Talbotson. When you and your wife came to the office last week in preparation for surgery, I said that yes, it is usually a simple procedure.

71

The complication would be if we found any extensive damage once we began. Mr. Talbotson, it was far worse than any of the pictures showed us. We did the best we could. Her heart couldn't take the pressure. I am sorry. But…she won't suffer any longer. She is in a better place now."

"Says who? Her better place was with me!" His mind filled with a torrent of pictures, memories, arguments, and vacations with the kids and the grandkids. He was both confused and apprehensive. He had no color left in his face. He had sipped the orange juice the nurse had brought a moment before. It had no taste. He didn't even feel it as it slid down his throat into an empty stomach. His stomach churned as the acid ate away at his stomach lining. He felt the juice and the acid make the return trip north. It stopped as far as his throat as the bile burned inside of him. He felt the bile rise into his very being, his soul. He buried his face into his hand, leaned over and began to sob. With tears streaming down past his chin and onto his shirt, he looked at the doctor. "What do I do now?"

The doctor never learned to separate herself from these situations. She wasn't sure it was a good thing or not, but her emotions helped her become the doctor that others wanted to emulate. With tears in her eyes, she put her arm around Mr. Talbotson's shoulder and squeezed him. "You have a family that surrounds you. You need to call them. They need to come here and help you say good-bye and make arrangements. If you like, I can call them for you."

"No, thank you, doctor. This is something I have to do. They are walking around the neighborhood trying to keep occupied until the surgery was over. I told them I would call them. They were driving me crazy just hovering over me. Doctor Schiffman, thank you for giving her the extra two years of her life. I suppose that it was time. Go and do your doctor job. Go give hope to another family." He leaned over and kissed her on the cheek as a grandfather would kiss a precious granddaughter. She blushed and cried while trying to put on a smile.

She stood up and walked down the corridor. He noticed that other people were walking past him on there way somewhere, perhaps to give somebody the news that they feared the most or to share with them the happy news of everything worked out just fine, that there was nothing to worry about.

As much as his family prodded, he hadn't left their house, Sheila's house since the funeral. Where was there to go? His kids and the neighbors kept bringing him food and the newspaper was still going to be there every morning at six.

The water continued to drip and the flag across the street continued to flutter in the breeze. Nothing changes. Nothing is the same. The sun rises in the morning and sets in the evening. It rises in the east and sets in the west. He thought nothing but mundane thoughts. Should he get up out of his chair in their Florida room, the enclosed porch that was good all year round? Should he sit here and wait until all the thoughts meshed into nothingness and there was no more to hear or see, smell, taste or touch? He no longer had answers, he could no longer make the simplest of decisions, but he didn't want anyone making decisions for him either.

As he looked out of the picture window in the front of the house, he listened to John William's Art of Guitar, a classical CD that he and Sheila would listen to on Sunday mornings after church while reading the papers. Tears would well up as he listened to the CD this first Sunday after her death. There would be no church any more though. Until this point, he believed. He fervently believed up until two years ago when Sheila was first diagnosed with a rare form of cancer. Dr. Schiffman had promised nothing. There would be a variety of options, but the short-term outcome would nonetheless be the same. There were radical options and there were the make her comfortable options. With a degree of temerity they chose the radical. They were people who chose risk over surrender. They researched on the Internet, they asked questions and they asked god for his advice and help.

The pain was long and she endured a great deal, my beautiful Sheila. It was at this point that my faith became questionable. At church, he prayed for her health, her life and her freedom from pain. But he began to question his wisdom. For what purpose does our god, our spiritual provider, our savior, and our maker of this world look down on the goodness of my Sheila and dole out such punishment? To what degree is this necessary? Is it not enough that there are continents engulfed in pain and suffering, war and starvation, plague and pestilence to keep him busy? Sunday after Sunday he would ask these questions and more. He questioned why an all-powerful and all knowing being would have pain and suffering, war and starvation, plague and pestilence. It was no longer about god and Sheila. This was bigger. This was philosophical. He began to see what he thought liberals would think, not the conservative that he was. That is of war and religion and their remarkable ties to each other. To him it was brief and succinct; war might be over land and as a result the deprivation of a people. He began to obsess over these notions. Was this the question for the ages? Has religion been used as the right to steal or gain what others have? Has religion been used to persecute and prosecute others? Has his life been nothing more than that of a sheep in the fold? He looked around at the other sheep in the flock and wondered what they thought. Did they think like he did now or like he did before? What was so strong in the appeal that brought them to god and to this holy place of worship?

He would sit with his laptop in the hospital lounge while Sheila received treatments using his wi-fi looking up religions around the world. He noticed the nearly parallel beliefs of his Jewish brethren and wondered if they had doubts. He noticed the symmetrical lines between the Passover Seder and the last supper of Jesus. He looked up Islam and Buddhism and continued to ask questions of himself. He began to ask questions of his parish priest. He asked questions of the rabbi in the town's synagogue. He drove to a moderately populated Muslim neighborhood and sought out the Imam. He found neither solace nor solid answers to sway him back to the fold.

William Talbotson, originally of Queens, New York and now of small town, Long Island had discovered his elusive thing. This would be the object to plague him for the remainder of his days. He set himself on a quest to save his wife and to save his soul in that order.

He started his research on the Internet and found a great article by writer Bruce Stevens, a Washington Post World Affairs Correspondent that began like this:

Has the deeply seeded beliefs in the existence of God created the turmoil, pain, and misguided stratagem that has led to the world in which we live; a world where man fights against man simply because of a conviction that their god is the true god, the true redeemer for mankind?

If we look through history, beginning at any point, we find religious tumult in communities, villages, and countries. Can we as a people reconcile the Spanish Inquisition or the Crusades? Was there a grand purpose aside from supremacy and authority of the Church?

We know, although Iran's President and Nazi Supremacists across the United States and Europe would deflect such statements, that German's attempted destruction of a people was nothing more than genocide. In the past decade there has been the attempted genocide of Bosnians and Serbians as well as Africans on the subcontinent. It has been nothing more than an attempt to hail their beliefs as irrefutable and dominant at the expense of what they would consider the *weaker population*.

So, let us take a look at the Iraqi policy that began with faulty information and ignorance on the part of the Bush administration. Is there any doubt that President George W. Bush has made the assault against an independent and sovereign nation anything more than a religious war? It could be viewed as such. Good vs. evil and God vs. Satan. The characteristics are there to make the argument.

Equally, Saddam Hussein told Iraqis: "Fight as God ordered you to do." So does this constitute a religious war, Christian versus Islam? This author would tend to lean in that direction.

He was not alone in his thoughts. There were others like him who felt the same way. They had the same questions, the same ideas and beliefs. There were conflicts in belief and in thought and they were not just his. He felt that he had been led by a leash all of his life and was like a racehorse who needed to wear blinders in order to be kept on the path of righteousness and goodness. He became angry with himself and then of his parents. How could they have been so blind—he believed everything they had taught him. He did what he was supposed to do and there was the statement that put it all in perspective for him. *He did what he was supposed to do!* Where was independent thought and reason? Where was the inner thought and balance where corporeal beings inherently know the difference between right and wrong?

He scanned the pages of religious wars and came up with centuries old battles. Of course there was the Crusades, The French Religious Wars in the latter part of the 16th century. Spain fought their religious wars during the same time and then there was the Thirty Years War from 1618—1648, which involved much of Europe fighting over Catholicism, Calvinism and Protestantism. *Religion clearly kills people,* he thought. And of course the friends of his generation never stop talking about the holocaust and the Nazi bastards who perpetrated such heinous acts against mankind. Where was the Jewish god then? Where was our god then? Where was anybody's god? Our spiritual creator, our benevolent benefactor and creator of the world; where were they, he, she, it, when millions were massacred because of their religious beliefs?

Then of course there were the Crusades and the nearly two centuries of warring among Christians and Muslims for control of Jerusalem. And of course, we should not forget the Spanish Inquisition. Religious war, ethnic cleansing seemed to be ubiquitous. He could of kept going on; Sudan, Darfur, Kosovo, etc., etc!

He grew tired. He closed his laptop and closed his eyes and waited for Sheila to finish her treatments. At last she came out looking weary and grey. They stopped in the hospital cafeteria for a cup of coffee before they left Manhattan for the drive back to the Island. They walked slowly hand in hand up the avenue to the parking lot where Bill raged inside as he saw the price for the parking lot. He passed over the money and walked away calling them thieves. "You should be ashamed of yourself charging so much money for a piece of concrete!" Sheila shushed him and said, "Bill, please. Don't make a scene. I just want to go home and go to sleep." "I'm sorry, honey. You're right." But he wasn't done because he knew she wasn't right. He was handed the receipt and they walked away to await some illegal immigrant to bring their car to the front of the garage. He didn't mind the illegals, they had to make a living and protect their families. It was the guy who owned the garage. He looked at the man behind the bulletproof window as they walked away. He pointed at him and silently mouthed the word, *thief.* It was childish, immature, but he felt a hell of a lot better.

XI

Billie awoke to the sounds of absolute silence. She reached across and found an empty space. She stretched, yawned and gently lifted her frame out of the bed. She ambled a few steps to the bathroom and brushed her teeth and ran a damp towel across her face. She looked closely at her face and was satisfied that she could face the world, if only for a short time. She proceeded to walk down the hall and down the carpeted stairs to the sitting areas downstairs. She found him reading there with a book in his lap and talking to their friends, Matt and Lori. It was her husband's last minute idea to book a trip to Block Island. Billie thought that it would be a great idea to invite their friends to go along. They sat together thinking back on the night before. It was the very face of theater, the sign of comedy and the sign of tragedy, fused together and inseparable as if it were yin and yang.

They had made the trip out from the island's East End to spend a day or two of quiet time away from the world. Block Island seemed the closest and yet most remote place of all and they were not disappointed. The only real disappointment came when they arrived for the 11:00 ferry at 10:58 and were turned away. They had to kill four hours in a place that had two restaurants open. They found a bar restaurant, whose name would escape them later, their favorite kind that overlooked the fishing vessels in the harbor. By the time they were sitting on the padded seats of the ferry, their laughter overtook the noise of the engines. Billie drank what she called troublemakers. A shot of 1800 Tequila in a bottle of Corona. Lori joined her while Matt and Mark drank Knob Creek, one of their favorite bourbons.

On board the ferry, they all drank beer out of cans. Lori reminded Billie about their high school days when the term of the day was "track ass." This was how they would get caught cutting class by their teachers. While cutting class, many kids would go and smoke a joint and bullshit, but they didn't have the sense to sit anywhere but the railroad tracks. Hence, when they returned to school, they had the imprint of the railroad tracks' grease on the seat of their pants. It took them a while to figure out that teachers were actually smarter than their students. Billie told them of the time her parents were struggling to make ends meet and decided to buy an inexpensive brand of laundry detergent. One after the other, Billie and her two sisters made their way to the school nurse, scratching, whining, tearing at their skins as the welts grew to great proportions. When the girls' mom finally came up to school to get them, she was exasperated. "Now I'm going to have to buy the good detergent and wash all of your clothes all over again." The sight of Billie struggling to scratch herself like a monkey had Lori, Matt and Mark nearly on the floor.

The inn was beautiful. It had six separate bedrooms with a bathroom in each. Each room had a balcony and a view in all directions. Billie and Mark's room had a view of the bare trees through which they could see the point in the harbor to their right and a pond directly ahead of them. There was a kitchen that overlooked one of the many ponds on the island. Like the living room and den on the first floor, all three rooms were of muted colors. The furniture was of mixed variety and of mixed coloring, all muted and calm as was the beige carpet with a muted red flowering pattern throughout.

Mark and Matt sat at the kitchen table, a table that would hold eight guests comfortably. It was their luck that they were the only four people booked at the inn. In fact, they would be the last customers of the season as it was the last week of October. With their temporary home to themselves and the warm welcome they received from Barbara, the proprietor of the inn, they made themselves quite at home in the dining room. Mark took large glasses from a nearby table and filled them with ice from the freezer. In each, Matt poured a healthy amount of bourbon, with a splash of vermouth and a couple of cherries—a fine Manhattan. Matt and Mark only knew each other for a few years, through their wives of course, and become fast friends. They became like brothers and each time out was a new and hilarious experience. Matt considered himself, especially after a couple of drinks, to be a reincarnated Viking. His famous phrase before slamming glasses together would be, *"Tonight we drink! Tomorrow we fight!!"*

The more that they drank, the more they became cerebral, which in of itself was a scary prospect; and they had been drinking since missing the ferry hours earlier. Matt was a two-time cancer survivor. He had just finished his last round of chemotherapy the week before and as strongly as Billie and Mark needed to get away themselves, they knew that Matt and Lori needed to get away and celebrate their new life together—again.

As Matt talked about his survival and his change of philosophy of life and priorities, Mark talked about his fears since recently suffering from a heart attack in his office. They were both in their forties and here they were trading war stories as if they were roommates in a nursing home. So they continued to sip their beverage of choice while Lori and Billie napped upstairs in their rooms.

When they came downstairs sometime later, they were shocked, but not surprised. "So this is what happens when we leave you two idiots alone?" Lori announced. "You are like two little boys getting their hands caught in the cookie jar." The only response they could come up with or that was worth responding with was in unison—*"Tonight we drink! Tomorrow we fight!!"*

So Billie and Lori sat down at the large dining room table with their own remedy of vodka, cranberry juice and pineapple juice. Within minutes, the laughter was contagious. Barbara, the inn's owner, without drinking, joined us from her apartment and made a few suggestions for dinner at nearby restaurants and laughed along with the off colored comments from both couples, especially, but not surprisingly, by the wives.

Lori and Billie continued to talk about their childhood. Billie remembers Lori's mother with her thick Spanish accent and strict regiment requesting of her husband to kill their daughter. She would state calmly but with dogged determination, "Harry, kill her. I want her dead". It came out as "Haarey, keel her. I want hur dedd" and they reeled with laughter. Lori remembers a hot summer night sleeping over at Billie's house where they claim the temperatures reached into triple digits in the upstairs of the small cape. After complaining enough times about being thirsty, Billie had gone downstairs to the kitchen and filled a large cooking pot with ice water. She brought it upstairs to Lori with a ladle and told her to drink until she drowned in it. This brought more laughter and of course, more to drink.

Dinner to Matt and Mark was nothing more than a blur. Matt had announced that the food sucked. The problem was not only hadn't they eaten, they hadn't yet ordered. Their wives at this stage were embarrassed and asked the waitress to make everything to go and hustled their husbands to the car. There was more *tonight we fight and tomorrow we drink or vice versa*, they cared little, which seemed apparent to the other patrons. Although somewhat mortified, they laughed along with their husbands as they sent them out to warm up the car and wait in the backseat. Mark and Matt were told in the morning that they had eaten back at the inn and fell fast asleep. Matt was told that he ordered a steak and not a moment later repeated his order because he forgot he had already done so.

XII

Mark rose early the next morning, leaving his wife sleeping blissfully in their warm, comfortable room. He sat at the dining room table with a collection of poetry by T.S. Eliot. He remembered there was a particularly long poem about religion, god and the building of churches, but he couldn't remember the name. He and his Uncle Bill were very close. They spoke on the phone usually once each week but emailed each other more frequently. His uncle was going through a very tough time dealing with the cancer of his wife Sheila. He was questioning the foundation of everything they had learned and believed in.

Mark had never had very strong feelings either way, never really getting involved in the argument of whether there was a god or not. He wasn't devout nor was he an atheist. He wouldn't even consider himself an agnostic. It generally wasn't on his radar, if you will. Yet his Uncle Bill was facing his own demons, he was fighting inwardly with the rock, the immovable and unwavering belief in his Christian faith. That was the name of the poem; *Choruses from "The Rock"* that he intended to read. He skimmed down the Table of Contents until he found the poem he was looking for.

Before sitting to read, he grabbed a cup of tea from the container of flavored teas behind him. He filled it with hot water and sat down facing the blustery October morning. It was grey and misty, with a stiff breeze. The empty tree branches swayed with the wind, moving as a conductor moves his arm and baton to lead the awaiting orchestra. Better still, it looked as if there were a puppeteer above them pulling and tugging on the strings to move the branches and limbs in a circular motion. Sitting at the bird feeder on the grey wooden deck was a red winged blackbird. It felt no emotion, no need to seek out some elusive thing. It didn't need to seek out a lover except during mating season, and then it was mating, not love making. It looked for no higher being, had no particular calling, no particular place to go or to be at any given time. It simply needed to eat. It needed to eat in order to survive. Its goal, though it wouldn't know it, was to survive the call of nature, to survive the food chain. Had Mark been able to write poetry, there certainly would have been some piece that he could have created that would be worthy of showing his wife and friends. As it was, he could write, but not poetry. Mark was a history professor at Stony Brook University where part of his responsibility was to write. He wrote for history journals, for Internet journals and had written a treatise on the impact of reactionaries during the presidency of Theodore Roosevelt. He was nearly finished with his first historical novel on the role of spies during the Civil War.

With his tea in place and a warm apple muffin prepared earlier by Barbara, Mark sat down to read and reread again T.S. Eliot's poem. He remembered it being somewhat contradictory and offering arguments from both sides. As a history professor, this is probably why he enjoyed this particular piece so much. In one swoop, opposing opinions and arguments could be formed and then be brought to close. This was how Billie thought, too. Her work as a criminal prosecutor taught her to look at every piece of evidence from every point of view. There were no margins for error. Her cases could be won or lost on a single mistake on a document, a piece of evidence that was marked inaccurately. Crime scene photos needed to be viewed and reviewed with monotonous repetition to ensure timelines and to help create and weave a story for the jury. The testimony of police officers, forensic scientists and victims had to be tested for veracity and needed to be thorough. No holes were allowed in any of her cases.

Like her husband, Billie needed to create a picture for the audience. Mark's picture was created with fact and thorough research and investigation. His students loved his classes because it was if they were spending a couple of hours or so at the theater. History was brought to life dramatically. Billie's audience was more critical and hopefully more thoughtful. The future of the victim was at stake. Would he or she be able to see that justice was served for them and for all of society?

Mark sipped his tea and put his pencil down along with the book and thought about the first time he and Billie had met. He was taking an elective course in law which he thought would help him at some point in doing research for what he thought would be a slew of books that he would write some day. He was interested in the critical analysis of digging deep and looking wide. Billie, with long flowing brown hair sat a few rows ahead of him. She was doodling on a pad and didn't seem at all engaged in the lecture by the law professor. I had lost interest a few classes back and started focusing my energies on meeting this girl. My time was used to find a way to get her to notice me without me being too obvious. For her part, Billie had sensed the same thing and had begun to move closer to where this curly haired guy was sitting near the back of the lecture hall. He was cute with great teeth. He could be someone I could get to know, she thought. Soon she was just to the front and to the right of him so that he could see what she was doing. She was drawing a picture of a guy. It was more of a doodle than anything else. It wasn't going to get into the Museum of Modern Art, but had she been five it would have made it to her parents' refrigerator.

It was now or never. Well never is too long term, but now seemed right. "Boyfriend?" he asked. She looked back at him, looked down at her doodle and then back up to him. She smiled. She looked somewhat embarrassed but with just a hint of flirtatiousness. "If you're lucky," she answered.

Class was over ten excruciating minutes later. He stepped over and asked if she wanted to get some coffee.

"I'm done with classes for the day. Maybe I'll let you buy me a beer," she responded.

He smiled, "If I'm lucky?"

"Yeah, something like that."

Two years later, Billie Holiday Pelton became Mrs. Billie Talbotson, husband of Mark who was nephew to Bill Talbotson, which reminded him of T.S. Eliot and the book that lay before him. He found the page he needed and began to read *Choruses from the Rock*.

As he read the piece, he jotted down some notes on a legal sized pad that he thought were pertinent and would be most beneficial to his Uncle Bill. Later on he would email much of his thoughts to his uncle.

Death is inevitable

There is both thought and action—a circuitous notion

Has man's growth in intellect led to his peace of mind? no!

Man has knowledge of gods word and yet he is ignoring gods word

Loss of faith—ignorance?

What have we given up for materialism? Death still waits for us at the end

Man's intellect has grown!

The more we know, the less we learn? What value is placed on the knowledge? Whose values?

Has man's faith subsided over time and has materialism and possession replaced faith?

Has man's ignorance caused him to fall from grace, from a reality that has god in their lives?

Greed, envy, avarice—what is it that makes man happy?

(ADDITIONAL THOUGHT—WASN'T THERE GREED, ENVY AND AVARICE WHEN THE CHURCH REINED SUPREME? SEEMS TO BE HYPOCRACY)

Spending money—Take a chance? Expecting reward is not guaranteed—but it is expected

What is it that man wants from life?

Eliot talks about change—priorities change but good and evil

Continue to struggle

Heaven and hell—god and satan

Yin and yang

Man's vagaries and emptiness surrounds us all

Successful people in spite of church

Or because of church? (Does it really matter)

Is Eliot talking about the expanded mind because of religion due to the fact that there are less blinders—people have a focus in church? (I don't buy this! Can religion narrow your mind because of the blinders? Possibly—less open and critical thought—just my opinion)

Perhaps the next generation can bring god back to the people—this was written in 1934—the questions remain today in the 21st century

Eliot talks about the community—the church used to be the cornerstone of each community—now it serves as a building to the few—how much has changed in seven decades?

Thinking only of himself/herself—why?

Vanity—materialism—(because people are human—this is human nature, isn't it?)

Eliot speaks of choice—choice is the Human element—Lost faith—lost values

He talks of materialism—So it would seem then, that being with god and enjoying your life must be mutually exlusive?! (Many would obviously argue this point—that being with God is enjoying your life)

Back to materialism and money—This is what we have evolved into—intellect and free will—so what is the problem?

Top of the page—I wrote that death is inevitable…

but if death is inevitable, Why are our actions and successes and

Enlightened minds diminished in value because some spiritual being is not involved in the human spirit?

Escaping death—what dreams? What darkness? Soul of man?

Fear of the unknown?

Jealousy of others? Fear of others?

Mans' choice—we have been given the intellect to reason, to create and to destroy—thinking for themselves—thinking for ourselves

Looking at the dark side of man—is this because man has stopped believing or is it because man is man who struggles with his own demons rather than imagined ones? Then, what are the imagined ones? Actual demons? Streams of consciousness? Conscience?

Looking to god for help when it was man who put themselves in the position in the first place. We try moving forward intellectually but end up falling behind when man does not take responsibility for themselves—what of accountability?

Can the human being survive and be sustained without faith or some sort of belief system?

This is man's very essence—to create, to build, to develop from nothingness into something

Is it that human kind must latch on to something even if it cannot be seen? Do we or must we praise that what cannot be seen to validate our existence, our lives, our past and our future?

He thought perhaps he needed to take some of his own advice and reread the work again. He began to imagine how he would put this together in a way that would help his uncle put things into perspective. Was it about mans' loss of faith? The loss of faith in a higher being or was it losing faith in humanity? Or, both? Knowing that death is the ultimate end is not an answer, but a reality. It is up to each individual to face that reality in a way, and in a spirit that makes sense to him or her. As man has grown in intellect, the need to create questions regarding all things tangible and not, existential and not become the order of the day—so why not question God, or question whether in fact there is one or not?

Eliot talks about sowing as the focal piece rather than the harvest. Is he asking us to think about what we want out of our lives or is he stating that doing what is right and just is the utmost of importance and that the end is nothing more than the end? It is inevitable. What we want out of life versus how we live our lives.

Later Eliot talks about the other side of death. What is waiting for us on that other side? He reread section three and he thought that god was angry and sarcastic. Look what I have given you and this is how you pay me back? But if there is a god, or some spiritual being, he has given man choice. Choice is free will—how does man use it over the millennia? Then why believe? Can't we live without church, without synagogue, without mosques? Can't we live on human values, core human values and dreams? But then someone would inevitably ask, *if not god, then where do these core values, these human values originate?*

By this time, Billie, Lori and Matt came slowly down the stairs and into the dining area, Matt grunting a good morning before grabbing a cup of coffee and a muffin. Mark put aside his work with relief and looked forward to a relaxing day with great people. This was supposed to be a brief respite from work; he felt as if he was beginning to take himself too seriously. Matt, a studio musician and owner/operator of a number of recording studios in New York City needed these days to relax. His wife, Lori, an OBGYN and clinical psychologist had taken some time off to help Matt with the chemo and Billie's work as one of the counties' top prosecutors, particularly needed some time away from the brutal case that she was working on.

XIII

Billie's case was an excruciatingly painful one for her. She never experienced anything like it in her career. Her colleagues had prosecuted similar ones, but so far, she had missed the opportunity and was thankful for it. It was particularly vicious and unnerving and she was going to be the biggest bitch she could be to lock up this animal.

On trial was a man in his late sixties who was molesting his young granddaughter and grandson. It had gone on for two years before one of the children finally stood up to him and told him no. The granddaughter then told one of her friends; the one she knew would believe her. Her friend in turn told her parents who anguished over making the phone call to their friends. But the fact was, what was important here or rather who was important here? "Kids come first," they had always said.

Billie's very purpose in life at this time was nothing short of figuratively, and literally in her dreams, to see this man's balls ripped off in a public square and pushed down his throat until he choked on the realization of what he did to these children, this family, this community and this civilization. She wanted him to be the poster boy for all other predators like him; to see that justice would be served, and that it would be swift and it would be punitive. She wanted others to actually see and feel the life sucked out of his very being, his very soul. Milton's seventeenth century poem, *Paradise Lost,* would repeatedly come to her in her dreams.

Nine times the Space that measures Day and Night
To mortal men, he with his horrid crew,
Lay vanquished, rolling in the fiery Gulf,
Confounded though immortal. But his doom
Reserved him to more wrath; for now the thought
Both of lost happiness and lasting pain
Torments him; round he throws his baleful eyes
That witnessed huge affliction and dismay
Mixed with obdurate pride and steadfast hate.
At once, as far as Angels ken, he views
The dismal situation waste and wild,
A Dungeon horrible, on all sides round
As one great Furnace flamed; yet from those flames
No light; but rather darkness visible
Served only to discover sights of woe,
Regions of sorrow, doleful shades, where peace
And rest can never dwell, hope never comes
That comes to all; but torture without end
Still urges, and a fiery deluge, fed
With ever-burning Sulphur unconsumed.
Such place Eternal Justice had prepared
For those rebellious, here their Prison ordained
In utter darkness, and their portion set,
As far removed from God and light of Heaven
As from the Center thrice to the utmost Pole.
Oh, how unlike the place from whence they fell!

Since death would not be an option in this case, she prayed that a prison sentence would manifest itself as the prison hell does here in just this one verse of the epic poem. Then she would be satisfied. But there was a great deal of work ahead of her. Depositions, pictures, social histories, psychological evaluations, all of which had to be conclusive, which would then enable her to weave a story of pain and suffering to the jury, that no compassionate or reasonable person could be dissuaded from.

Lori had been called upon as an expert in the field of sexual assault. When any such case came about, she was paged wherever she was in the hospital and brought down to a special area so that she could perform, tactfully, the tests that were required. There was no margin for error in the medical field, so she used that same approach in these cases because they were to become legal cases, where the margin of error translated into acquittal or conviction. The results were conclusive on Lori's end. This was just one piece, a major piece, of an intricate puzzle that needed to be examined from every direction. Like a puzzle, you must get up out of your seat and view the pieces and its placement from all sides of the table. Several child psychologists were also called into work with the children and help them move forward. There would be many months and years ahead of family counseling and individual counseling.

Typically, she and Mark would sit down to dinner together, whenever their schedules allowed, and she would run through her cases out loud to see if there were any holes. Mark would listen as if it were a historical piece. He would help her craft the story and help her pick out nuances that might peak the interest of a member of the jury. This case was very different. There was a biting anger, a disgust that welled up from within her very being. There was never an excuse for this time of heinous crime. He would pay, and pay dearly. She didn't know yet at what cost it would come.

XIV

Weeks after their trip to Block Island, Mark continued to look up items that might inspire his uncle. His uncle continued to serf the web at the hospital as he waited for the poisonous chemicals to surge through his wife's veins searching for and destroying all remnants of the cancer that slowly crept through her body so that she would be strong enough for the heart surgery. They would email each other until the day that Sheila passed away. It was inevitable, her death. Ideas were no match for the inevitable toll of life.

Bill was not a historical buff like his nephew, but it helped give him focus. He didn't necessarily relate his current situation to those of the past, but it was important for him to see if others believed what he was trying to come to terms with—that god was nothing more than a creator of the planet. He left the tools, the chemical enzymes, the proteins and building blocks to see that the planet would evolve. He came to believe that it was the ultimate oxymoron: creative evolution. If you were a strict believer in the construction of things, much like many supreme court justices, then you literally believed that on the first day, god created...on day two...and so on until he created man...then gave him a plaything...well two playthings, one of his own and then Eve.

At this point, god cracked open a beer, sat back, belched and said, this is going to be good. He hung around for a couple of million years, tinkering here and there, played around with the cosmos for a while, and would visit other galaxies and worlds and come back every now and then to see what developed. God was the ultimate television executive. He had his hand in things but never directly involved. He would give a no comment here and there and couldn't be found at other times, i.e., the holocaust, the crusades, etc., etc., blah, blah, blah.

He came back during a commercial break during another planet creation far off in the galaxy. There were dinosaurs walking, crawling, and flying everywhere. He stayed around for a while and then got bored. Here is where the story gets interesting. He couldn't make up his mind as to how to cancel this series. He thought of a planet crushing asteroid or giant meteor shower that would envelope the planet. From there, dark clouds of poisonous gasses would block the suns rays, causing there to be no food grown. The carnivorous bastards would eat up all of the liberal pansy assed vegetarians until there was nothing left. They would look around at each other, gasp and say, shit, we fucked up big. How will we fix this? They were republicans so they couldn't fix it. They just blamed each other and became extinct. Next.

Somehow or other, he came back to the Adam and Eve thing and watched this play out. He toyed with them as they toyed with each other. Bill believed that god was the penultimate storyteller. He set the stage and then let the writers do their magic. He came up with the symbol of comedy and tragedy and placed it in the back of some schmuck's mind that claimed to come up with the design. "Ungrateful bastard," god said to himself. "I shall smite you." And he did. Probably killed by a hit and run chariot driver.

Bill grabbed himself another coffee in the cafeteria, sat back down and started typing out his ideas in word pad. He would later email this to his nephew who would get a kick out of it.

So now the cosmic writers penned their new character Eve as a temptress. Dark hair, dark eyes with a great figure. Adam was smitten. Nobody uses that word, he thought to himself. Adam wanted to the bang the hell out of her. She was being coy, playful, flirtatious and hard to get. She had this whole kinky snake and apple thing going on that he couldn't figure out. But he wasn't evolved enough to understand her. (One of Bill's first girlfriends in high school said that same thing to him once). Adam just wanted to get her behind a tree in the orchard somewhere. She had his full attention, both figuratively and literally. It wasn't long before they fucked up the world. The Christian Right and Conservative movement would say that, not in quite those words, but that was the gist of it. Bill laughed out loud and then realized where he was. He smiled to those around him. It was the first time that he had laughed or smiled in some time.

Mark returned the email a couple of days later. He felt better that is uncle wasn't being as depressing as he had in his last emails.

Uncle Bill,

Glad that you had a laugh at the expense of the human race. I can tell you that these little thinking out loud sessions you are holding for yourself will do you a world of good. It is better than reading about witchcraft and the age of enlightenment. And it is certainly better than the genocide you were talking about during the St. Bartholomew's Day Massacre and the death of the 50,000 Huguenots. A little depressing, don't you think?

How is Aunt Sheila doing today? I hope it goes better than the last round of treatments did.

Billie has been really busy at work lately. She is working on something that is really getting to her. She hasn't brought it up, but it is tough. That's the hard part to understand though—she always tells me about her cases. She runs them out loud to me so I can help her script them. Not this one. I'm sure she'll tell me when she is ready. BTW, she sends her regards.

I've got my one of my classes working on a paper about god and religion. Has religion shaped history or has history shaped religion? We've been talking about parallels in Judeo-Christian beliefs and its progress forward, or lack of progress depending on your view...the student's view. A couple of students are working on Islamic beliefs and how it has evolved into what we see on the news today as opposed to what many believe it should look like. I'm looking forward to reading the papers in a couple of weeks. The discussions have been great. I have been sharing some of our emails to help make this more realistic to them. That this isn't a discussion based on a syllabus but a conversation that is held daily. An intellectual debate.

I will pass on the interesting ones to you. Uncle Bill, there are many, MANY people who feel like you do.

Anyway, I've got class in ten minutes. I have to get out of the office and over to class.

Talk later.

Love,

Mark

XV

Katie and I drove over to the docks during our recent Nor'easter. The waves crashed against the concrete, which was the only thing that stopped the onslaught of water from hitting the catering hall that nestled up against the inner bay. You couldn't tell where the ocean ended and the parking lot began. We sat in our truck with a bottle of wine and a couple of plastic cups and admired nature's fury. At one point, the waves actually crashed over the truck. Fortunately it wasn't when Katie had the windows down and was taking pictures. She thought they would make a fine addition to the restaurant, near the bar. I didn't disagree.

We were not alone in the admiration department. Many trucks and cars made their way to the parking lot to catch the waves, so to speak. It was like watching an old black and white movie. Everything was grey. The sky was grey. The ocean was grey. The parking lot was grey. The mist and the spray from the crashing waves were gray. Like a black and white television set, the greys were different in contrast. The only thing that wasn't grey was our moods. We just sat and admired the view.

"I got a call from my cousin, Billie today," Katie stated. "You remember her, right?"

"Writer from Massachusetts".

"Lawyer from out east. Her husband is the history professor."

"Vaguely. Massachusetts, Connecticut, out east. No big difference. We're east too. Same continent. What's up with them?"

"Mark…" I gave the look of uncertainty until she made sure I was certain…

"Her husband…Mark's aunt is dying from cancer…"

"Who isn't?" I interrupted.

"She was wondering, since the aunt is Sheila Talbotson, the food critic, if we would hold a kind of memorial at the restaurant after the funeral. Whenever that is. Sheila has been the food critic for the local Long Island paper and a regular at Katie's Place. We had made Zagat's Review early on in our tenure as restaurateurs. When she wasn't working she would more than often bring a few of her friends and family members to dinner on a weekend. She was easy about the main dishes, but quite particular about her desserts. Cherry cheesecake or a chocolate mousse with a strong cup of coffee. One of the comments she had made about our restaurant was how a variety of smells were able to blend in to one another without being offensive. While garlic would be a lingering smell, enticing to the customers, in the background was the fresh and distinct presence of a rich coffee blend.

"Sure, that's fine. When was the last time you spoke with her? I haven't heard you mention her name in a while".

"We email each other a couple of times during the year. You know…just to keep in touch. We used to be much closer when we all lived closer to each other when we were younger. Then everyone just went their own ways when they got older."

"We haven't talked about what is going to happen when we die," Ryan said.

"I told you that I don't want to be buried. I don't want any bugs and worms crawling through me. I want to be cremated. You can spread my ashes over the ocean."

"Actually, I was going to sell them on EBay and see what I can get for you." Katie tried to smack me in the back of the head, but expecting this I deftly ducked away. "Me," I continued, "I want to be placed on a lounge chair at the ocean. I don't care what happens because sadly I will be dead and won't feel a thing or care even the slightest. The birds can eat my flesh and the bones can be washed to sea. Then the bones will come up washed upon some foreign shore. What better way to see the world." He took a sip of the wine and was promptly called an ass by his wife. Ah, love.

XVI

The funeral was cold and damp. A heavy mist hung in the air along with the heavy sadness that lingered and moved from mourner to mourner during the eulogy. We learned things about Sheila that we hadn't known before and of course the bright reminisces of things remembered. Tears flowed openly from those close while others on the periphery of her life had moistened eyes, the tears of fondness, the tears of sadness and the tears of what yet lay in store for them when they became older, or sick, or when life was taken away in the prime of someone's life; or their life.

Katie stood at my side and I was overcome with a darkness that I had felt creeping over me for sometime, but was reluctant to show its presence until it was ready. Today, it would seem, the shadow that hung over me chose this time to show its face to no one but myself. I didn't find this strange, but a welcome relief, an uncomfortable relief, but one nonetheless. It had hidden behind myriad webs in dark crevices during dreams I had while trying to sleep. They would be gone in the morning, but what remained was a disconcerting feeling that I couldn't place my finger on. I didn't yet share these feelings with Katie, because I didn't know what to explain or how to make her see what I saw. Rather, that was part of the problem. I didn't want her to see what I saw. It was Steven King like, and I had read enough of his novels to know that my internal reality would not be seen by others.

My dreams were in black and white, I'm not sure if all dreams are this way, but I began to recall these horrors in black and white, which seemed to me more destructive, more devastating, more realistic. Dark shadowy figures crept in and out of the corners of my mind. They had black masks that draped behind them into a cape. There was nothing else to wear. They were monsters that were neither male nor female. My dreams didn't lend themselves to their mating habits, but rather their feeding habits. They were vulture like, waiting for death, but death always surrounded them. They would hover above homes, above the trees in parks waiting for the inevitable. It was always night. Always night. Night above all else. Dark and foreboding. Dark and forbidding. Forbidden darkness. Forbidden entry to all that was light and seeing. For the victims of these caped demons, there was no escape. There were no pardons, no exceptions.

The fear came not of death, but knowing that death would not be restful. Would not be peaceful. It was dark and cold. There was the mist and the breath of the foul wind of hell. It could be summer and sultry and humid. It was cold and foul. The victims knew time was running out and that time was elusive and no measure of prayer or atonement could overrule the inevitable silent screams of the flesh ripped away from the skull and the soul torn from within as if a child torn from the hands of their parents by a psychotic bent on pain and torture. The screams were heard within their own ears and the pounding of the heart like a timpani in a philharmonic orchestra, keeping its own rhythm. Louder and louder, faster and faster, both the drumming and the screams from within.

The fear came not of death, but knowing that death would not be restful. Would not be peaceful. It was dark and cold. It was your turn to face the wrath of the unknown but known assailants sent from hell, shrouded in their black masks that flowed behind them like a cape. It was always your turn, and that in itself was the prize from hell. It was always your turn until it was actually your turn, and that timeframe was not presented to you. You received neither memo nor email from the cold mist and breath of the foul wind of hell. That was the punishment in black and white. There was no need for blood and gore, just waiting for the inevitable, the elusive timeframe for which no man nor woman could escape their just due.

These dreams didn't come at night any longer. They would find their way into the matrix of my imagination during the day. Today it found me during Sheila's funeral. There were voices around me but I heard no one. There was movement around me but I saw nothing. There was Katie taking my arm, but I didn't feel her. I felt darkness. I felt the hole that Sheila was being lowered into. Her eternal place of rest. Rest. Peace. I hoped. It couldn't be what I was living in my mind.

I shook of the darkness and despair that was taking hold of my mind, and I took hold of Katie and walked back to our car. I said nothing, but handed her the keys and walked around to the passenger side, where I silently sat, belted myself in and closed my eyes, half afraid to look at Katie for fear of her asking me what was wrong and half afraid of opening my mind to the demons in the black masks that flowed over what could be shoulders and fell behind them in a cape. It was dark and cold. It was night. It was always night. Clouds of grey blanketed whatever stars there might be in the heavens. There was the mist and the breath of the foul wind of hell. It was misty and rainy. It was cold and raw. I opened my eyes to daylight. It could have been sunny and sultry and humid, but it was cold and raw and we were in a place of death, a place of ending, of solitude, of aloneness. It was spiritual and spiritless.

I looked at Katie. She looked back. We hadn't driven anywhere although it felt as if we were in the car for hours. "I don't know how to help you unless you open up."

"I don't know what to say or how to say it".

"Honey, I hear you every night. I don't know what you are saying but I know that you are scared. Can you tell me about your dreams?"

"I'm not sure. I need a drink. I need more than a drink. I need help." Her simple reply of okay took the weight off because I knew intuitively that she knew what to do if I didn't.

XVII

Billie left the courthouse after asking for a temporary delay so that she could attend the funeral. The judge was not happy, but understood and granted her a two-day delay. She thanked his honor, packed up her files, gave the defendant a look that said, sit in jail and suffer a couple of days. Think about how I'm going to tear you apart, you miserable piece of shit. He did and so did she.

While Mark drove, she reviewed file after file and note after note. Mark looked over at her. "I've never seen you so focused on a case like this. What's so engrossing that you can't even be sarcastic and obnoxious about my driving?"

She sighed and looked at him. "I want to make sure that the bastard I am trying never sees the light of day for the rest of his miserable existence."

"Well, I'm glad that you are not taking this personally. I was scared for a minute. I thought I saw some legal emotion for a second."

She smacked him on the arm and smiled, realizing how personally she was taking this.

"So…?"

"This guy is in his late sixties. He has been molesting his grandkids and it just makes me sick."

"Most of the people you try make you sick, so what's the difference here? Sounds like it is a different version of the same pond scum you deal with daily."

"I had a friend growing up who went through the same shit and I saw what it did to her and her family. Some people believed, others didn't— and others didn't even want to know. They were too embarrassed to be associated with the family. This was one of the things that pushed me into law. I couldn't understand what made animals like this tick, so I figured rather than figure them out, lock 'em up on an island somewhere and let them practice on each other."

"Okay. It explains a lot lately."

"That noticeable?"

He gave her one of his patented *are you kidding* looks? "Alrighty then. Lets change the subject. Do we know what is going on after the funeral?"

"Yeah. A few of us with your Uncle Bill will be going to my cousin's restaurant to eat and drink. They don't open the restaurant until late in the afternoon, so we'll drive over after the funeral. The place will be ours until they open for regular business. You will like them. They're like us."

"Smart, intellectual, gorgeous, the upper crust of society. Martini drinkers with their pinkie fingers in the air." In his best aristocratic British voice, "Darling, it will be simply smashing, A marvelous time engaged in conversation with others as fine and distinguished as we are. Simply brilliant, darling. Simply brilliant."

And in her best redneck voice, "Sheeit, (shit), some Wiald (Wild) Turkey and corndogs. I wanna see how many teeth your uncle has left in his mouth. I reckon he ain't got no more than nian (nine)."

"Feel better?" he asked.

"Much better." She put the files into their folders and put them in her briefcase. "Pull over next chance you can. I think you need to make me feel much better." She reached across and started playing with Mark's hair.

"That would be smashing, darling. Brilliant and smashing. Hot damn, yall gonna get lucky now baby! This is more like it. That's what I'm talking about." Mark didn't need much encouragement and starting dancing in his seat looking for a suitable spot to make his wife feel better. What would be suitable on the Long Island Expressway? The service road.

XVIII

Bill knew this day was coming. He prepared for it. He researched god and religions. He thought about Buddhism for a while too. He remembered reading back in the sixties one of his favorite authors—Jack Kerouac. The Dharma Bums and a couple of others that had the characters getting high and getting laid all the time without any real responsibility. Hopping on trains, working on small temporary jobs to have enough to eat and drink. Sleeping out in the woods on the sides of the road in sleeping bags and catching their own food when necessary. It was about enlightenment and the Four Noble Truths. Removing greed, ego centeredness, and craving from one's life. He thought of even meditating and being aware of his breathing.

He had done some reading on these concepts and found that an interconnectedness among things in the world is one teaching. Buddha realized the truths during his experience of enlightenment. To discover the truth was to discover happiness. The purpose was to find and to have clarity of perceptions, reason and knowledge and to resist destructive temptation. Who were they kidding he thought to himself? Abstinence from worldly pleasures? What would be the point in living the full life— the Great American Dream? To connect to something greater than oneself. Well, I did that. I had Sheila.

In a nutshell, Buddha believed that human suffering stemmed from ignorance. Okay. I can see that. We're all fucking idiots looking for something better. His better was Nirvana. Being free from mind contaminants, like lust, anger, and craving. But lust is good. It keeps you young. And it isn't just a guy thing. Women have lust. They dream of boy toys don't they. Sheila loved to talk about some of her favorite baseball players. She didn't know what position they played or much cared what position. She just liked looking at them. Nothing wrong with that. That's what Playboy was for wasn't it? The great articles of course. The pictures were just the bonus, like the bubble gum in baseball cards.

He also found that the Americans in Kerouac's books were unlike the Buddhists across the world. So like anything else, there were different versions, different truths, different beliefs, values and spin put on the One True Truth. Sexual freedom was part of the Dharma Boys truths.

So now I am sitting here in the limousine parked in front of the gravesite for my beautiful wife, Sheila. So what did I learn from my research while passing the time while Sheila was wasting her time with poisons running through her body? I could say that life sucks and then you die, but I won't because it isn't true. I learned that I really don't have much faith in god or some being because of history, but I cannot ignore that there is a supreme being that had to have had a hand in the formation of this world. Could this world have just randomly developed amongst the billions of stars and rocks in the cosmos? I wasn't sure, but I didn't think so.

The door opened to the limo, and I found that it was time to face the reality. The end was here. It was time to say good-bye to my wife, my life, my partner, my soul mate. It was cold and raw with a mist. Perfect for the type of day it was. *Keeping inner peace in the face of stress*—maybe I picked something up from the Great Buddha after all. I found an umbrella over my head and family all around. It would be fine. After all, we are all connected, so says the Great Buddha.

XIX

Katie's Place opened earlier than usual, but today was not like any other day. There were connections here; connections previously established and connections not yet made based on the *Six Degrees of Separation*. I was in the back preparing some simple comfort foods while a small gathering of friends and family assembled along the bar. Katie tapped a keg and began pouring one of the favorite Long Island beers, Blue Point. Some of the Long Island wines were already poured into decanters and our guests were pouring freely among themselves. Along the bar Katie placed a bottle of Maker's Mark, a bottle of Johnny Walker Black, a bottle of Grey Goose, some vermouth, and assorted pieces of lime, lemon, olives and cherries. Our guests were encouraged to help themselves. I thought briefly of raising the prices on the dinner menu for a couple of weeks to recoup this gathering, but thought better of it after anticipating Katie's probable reaction.

The lights were kept low and the blinds partially shut to mimic the somber mood. It was a gathering of people who shared connections—it was not a party although Sheila would have preferred it to be so. Light classical music played in the background. Simple and soft chamber music—cellos and violins and violas. Soft enough not to be intrusive but grand enough to seep into the unconscious mind.

The dream I had last night came to me at once while I was listening to the music and the sounds of people familiar with one another speaking in various tones. I was supposed to drive someone a great distance, which I didn't mind, to then find out that I needed to go a greater distance to a different place first. I was angry and disturbed, but did what I was supposed to do. What I promised to do? What I was told to do? I knew the place that was the secondary location, a college town in upstate New York. In the next segment of the dream, I realized I had no car and the ride that I estimated to take eighteen hours in total became an unrealistic goal. I had to slide on a two-lane road in the darkness on my butt using my hands to pull me along the snow-covered asphalt. I wasn't the only one. I passed people along the way who either walked or pulled themselves along as I did.

After I realized that I was able to walk, I made better time. I looked for signs along the way to show me the right path or direction. In time, I came to a crossroad where people sat and rested for a time, waiting for others who were trying to make up their minds in terms of where to go and what to do. I thought about stealing a car from the parking lot, but there were too few and too many people. There was a pub where people were drinking beers. They were not permitted to be inside, so they stood around a fire in a barrel, making me think of homeless people under bridges in cities and towns across the United States. I wasn't homeless or an indigent, but I did feel like one. I was purposeless except for the fact that I had to get to this college town to drop someone off. But I had no one with me. The purpose and direction had already changed in the dream.

After a time, it seemed timeless though; I continued my travels along the snow-covered road until I reached a grey door in a narrow corridor where others waited patiently. It was there that I recognized a former employee that I needed to discuss a sensitive issue with. Sensitive to his continued employment. I was reluctant to do so because he was with his family. It seemed inappropriate to do so but I had waited too long already. I made pleasant conversation with him until I was ready to bring up the issue. At this point, the door opened and I found myself sitting in a grey station wagon facing the snow-covered streets. I wasn't alone in the car, but for all intents and purposes, I was. I couldn't speak or communicate. I could only watch. It was still dark.

The seat I sat in turned out to be an overflowing toilet that could not be controlled. Strange as it seemed, none of my co-passengers in the car that wouldn't move noticed. Everyone was oblivious to one another. They knew nothing but their own personalized dark thoughts and stories. Dreams that had their own special reality to them.

Katie walked over and pulled me aside. She asked where I was as she handed me a glass of wine. "Someplace weird. Thanks for bringing me back home. Freud would have had a field day with the dream I had last night."

"It must have been about sex. Id or ego or your mother. What is going on with you lately?"

"I'm not sure. I feel like I have lost focus on…on everything. Its weird. I have crazy dreams that seem like reality and during the day it feels as if I am sleepwalking through reality. Thanks for the wine."

"What do you want to do?"

"Let's go meet your cousins."

Katie and I walked across the room towards Mark and Billie who were sitting at a table talking quietly to one another. They looked up and smiled as we approached them. Billie stood up and said, "I was wondering when you two would come over and join us. It has been too long. How have you been?" She took my hand in hers and we shook politely.

"I've been good. Busy as you can see." I waved my hand around the room as if a museum curator. "We've been open now for just over a year. We should have done this long ago under different circumstances. How have you been?"

"Great. Busy as hell. But that isn't anything new. Let me introduce my husband Mark to you. Mark, this is Ryan. Ryan, Mark."

Great to meet you, Ryan. I've heard a lot about you. The place is great. The food is terrific."

"Thanks. Good to meet you, too. I hear you are a history professor. How do you like being on stage every day?"

"I love it. It is like being an actor. If you don't bring the dead to life for these kids its like talking to yourself for an hour at a time. It's like competing with Sesame Street. Every sixty seconds I have to change the graphics or the voice or something."

"So how has your uncle been?" Katie asked. "He seems to be handling it well."

"You know, I am not sure. I think he is okay today. He has had a lot of time to prepare himself for this, but once it comes you really never know how you are going to react. We have been emailing each other back and forth for some time now talking about god and religion. He has many doubts now because of this."

"Don't let him near Ryan. He will talk him out of religion by the end of the night," Katie said as a matter of fact.

"And what is wrong with that? God, to me, and I am not preaching or anything, just my own opinion and experience, God is nothing more than a brilliant story from the imagination of a brilliant and inspirational author. Historically speaking," and I looked towards our historian, Mark, "I feel as if it were a way to keep a group of people focused away from their troubles. It was a way to keep a wayward people together. But there was nothing real to it except in the mind of the storyteller and the willingness to believe by others. After that it was perverted by others for their own means."

"You know, you almost sounded brilliant until you became your usual cynical self," Katie quipped.

"Thank you darling. Who knows me better than you?" He leaned over and they kissed.

"Historically speaking, of course," Mark began, "religion has been intertwined in the uplifting of a people throughout the centuries. Look how Moses used religion and the notion of God to bring his people out of Egypt to be saved. Was it the story telling of Moses or was it the strength of a person to lead?"

Billie, with a glass of wine in her hand offered the following notion. "The question really could be whether Moses was a leader in his own right as a person with an inner courage and a moral compass to bring a beaten down people out of an ugly situation. Or was he an opportunist at the right place at the right time as others in history have been? Cheers to me. What do you think about that?"

"What about the fact that the Egyptians used religion as a means to segregate and break a people because of their God? Using religion to create a hierarchy."

"Similar to a caste system in India. Interesting."

"I am going to let you guys entertain yourselves for a while. Billie, lets get a drink and catch up. I've missed you, cousin." They walked away towards the bar leaving Mark and Ryan to their quest for answers. "Honey," Ryan called over, "Can you send over a bottle of our finest bourbon? We are going to be chatting for a while." Katie gave him her patented are your legs broken look, smiled and walked over and whispered into one of the waitress' ears.

Mark excused himself for a moment. "Ryan, I am going to bring my Uncle Bill over. He needs to be a part of this. Maybe this will get him refocused and get some closure. Excuse me for a moment." Mark crossed over a few tables where his uncle was in idle conversation listening to people tell him how sorry they were and how they will miss Sheila. "Uncle Bill, can I have a moment?" "Yes of course. Excuse me everyone. Thank god. Where the hell have you been? I can't listen to this anymore."

"Come over here and meet Ryan. He and his wife own this place. We've been talking and I thought you might want a bourbon and relax with us." After the introductions and a fresh pour, Mark told his uncle that they were talking about their emails.

"Have you now? So what do you think Ryan?"

"I think that I rather not taint the conversation until I hear from you. I have some very definite beliefs and I don't want you to not like me right away. I usually like to get people into a false sense of security before they don't like me."

"You sound upfront. I like that in a man. You also sound like a sarcastic son of a bitch. I like that, too. What are we drinking and what are we drinking too?"

"We are drinking Michter's, a very nice bourbon and we are drinking to you and to your life with Sheila."

"To my Uncle Bill and Aunt Sheila. Two people who found love and life together and made it last a lifetime." They raised their glasses, brought them together and sipped the warm, smoky brown liquid down.

"This is nice," Bill said as he looked at his glass. "I'm usually a Dewars guy, but this is good."

"Bill, later on we will go to my office in the back. I have my private stock of really good scotches and bourbons. I only take it out for special occasions and special people. This afternoon might just be one of those times."

"Well thank you. I might need it and it is greatly appreciated. Thank you for opening your restaurant to us."

"Whatever Katie wants I give her. If it is important to her it is important to me."

"Well, thanks again. Okay, God is it? I have had many thoughts and ideas since Sheila got sick. I spent a lot of time on my laptop researching on the Internet while sitting in the hospital waiting for her treatments to end. I had a lot of time to sit and think about life and people and God. Honestly, I am not sure what to think anymore."

"If I remember your earlier emails, you first brought up the subject of an existence of god when Sheila was diagnosed with cancer. As simply as I can make it was the argument that how could there be a god or supreme being when someone like Sheila can become so severely ill when the dregs of society can walk around unscathed."

"In a nutshell, yeah, that would be it. You read the newspapers and you see these animals walking around doing whatever they want and doing all kinds of stuff to people and they get to live a long life."

"Billy Joel," Ryan said between sips of bourbon.

Mark looked at him with sudden recognition. "Only the good die young." They raised their glasses to one another and silently cheered each other with a nod of recognition and newfound friendship.

"Sorry, I'm a Sinatra and a Brecker Brothers kind of guy. You guys really want to talk about God right now? I think of myself as kind of bright, but it is a little heady, especially today."

"Uncle Bill, because of what today is, it is more than appropriate to talk about it—that is of course if you want to. You don't have to if you don't want to."

"Its fine. I didn't want to impose my thoughts and troubles on anyone." He said this and looked in Ryan's direction.

"Bill, you don't have to worry on my account. Today is about you and what you need. If you need to talk about this, or yell about this, whatever you need to do is fine. To tell you the truth, I've some things going on in my head that this might be the perfect venue for. Besides it will save me a co-pay at some shrinks office. So by all means, go right ahead."

Bill was more comfortable now and began to talk at length about what he had read and what he thought about what he read. He talked about what it meant to him to be in the hospital sitting and researching about the various religions while Sheila lay with tubes of poison running through her veins. He felt a little disingenuous talking about Sheila without her sitting beside him, as he was accustomed. But this dialog began to be a catharsis for him. Ryan and Mark sat hunched over listening intently with Ryan sitting back every now and then to take everything in and see how it measured up to what he believed or didn't believe. They talked about the science of the parting of the Red Sea as opposed to the biblical miracle portrayed in word and on film.

Mark helped fill in the historical blanks for his uncle. They discussed medieval times along with the crusades and the quest for absolute power using the Church as a vehicle to control the masses.

Ryan interjected a thought. "So how different is it today with Churches controlling the people. Back in the seventies, you had the Reverend Moon and his Moonies with mass weddings and vans on corners trying to convert stupid teenagers, myself included. Is he still alive? Anyway, what about Billy Graham and the adulterant minister with the wife and the makeup—what the hell was her name?"

"Tammy Faye, I think. I can't put my finger on his name. Baker?"

"Yeah, maybe. That reminds me—when I'm done being blasphemous, I want you to try some Bakers Bourbon. Great stuff. Anyway, Baker or whoever it was had all these brainwashed people in the palm of his hands. He was collecting money from them left and right. Blind Faith. A snake charmer. Nothing to do with god—everything to do with what will happen to you if you don't believe in god and the church that fosters the belief."

"So you don't believe at all?" Bill asked.

"Basically, I am a cynic. I need you to show something to me. Because you said so doesn't work with me. What about you, Mark?"

"I've grown up with religion. Like Uncle Bill, it was all around. Did the Church thing, Christmas mass, etcetera. You know though, once you become an adult and have a mind of your own, that mind finds other avenues of thought." He stopped for a moment to contemplate the drink in his hand. He swirled it in his hands and admired the caramel color. "I'm still working on it. I have the rational thoughts that say, prove it and then I have that innate, I won't say irrational thoughts, that says you need to have faith; need to believe. I guess that I am still evolving."

"Interesting choice of words. Evolving?" Ryan stated with a quiet smile. "Where does the religious right fall in on the dinosaur thing?" he asked rhetorically.

"One point for Mr. Bourbon, our host," Bill stated while holding up his glass in a mock toast. Mark nodded in acknowledgement.

On the other side of the restaurant, Billie and Katie were talking about, well, just about everything. They talked about their marriages, they talked about their jobs and their families, they talked about shoes and handbags and they talked about shopping in general. It was the latter rather than the former that they began with. Of course they loved each other's shoes and wanted to know where they were purchased. Some in the city, some off the Internet and some down the road in the small Hampton's villages near where they lived.

Billie told Katie about their drive west across Long Island. "I'm sitting in the passenger seat reading files from the case I'm working on and I'm thinking, actually feeling horny. I made him pull over to the side under a overpass and we did it right there." She blushed and giggled and sipped some of the wine she had in her glass.

"Details my darling cousin. Supply me with the details and then I've got some stories for you. But I think we might need some more wine." She poured a glass for each of them.

Around the restaurant other family members and friends of Bill and Sheila made conversation, some similar, about religion, sex and life in general. Some were political and others spoke of the artwork and design of the restaurant. They noted the shades of colors and one blended into another giving off a comfortable aura. The artwork was in some cases complimentary and other pieces in stark contrast. It seemed they would say that the pieces belonged to Ryan and Katie more so than to the restaurant. It would appear as if they wanted their lives to show in the restaurant. Various pieces came from their vacations together across the United States, the Caribbean and Europe, especially Italy and Spain.

Throughout the short few hours that the mourners gathered, there would be groups of men together and groups of women together. Every now and then spouses would link up and join groups so that the conversation would change direction and spirit. Not in all cases though. Some of the raunchy conversations would become raunchier and the political more spirited as husbands and wives would complain about the others choice of political affiliation or affliction.

Billie and Katie eventually made their way over to their husbands where they were still engaged with Uncle Bill in the discussion of religious beliefs and how they each came to their current position. Uncle Bill was discussing why he thought he might become a Buddhist Monk.

"Uncle Bill," Billie began, "I kinda think that you're cut off. Buddhist Monk is usually the universal sign for the drinking is over." She smiled and leaned over and kissed him on the cheek. "Are these guys helping you out or do you need help from two beautiful women with brains?" Uncle Bill blushed at the attention.

"I could use some help from two beautiful women," Ryan suggested. His suggestion resulted in punch in the stomach from Katie and then her trademark smile. "How's that for help. Your turn Billie, this way he gets the full effect of our little ménage a trois."

"Not exactly what I was thinking, but okay."

Katie looked to her immediate guests at the table, and said, "Can you excuse us for a few minutes?" And with that, Katie and Ryan walked towards the kitchen and through the swinging doors. The bright lights of the kitchen immediately changed the mood and atmosphere.

"What's up, honey?" Ryan asked.

"That's what I wanted to ask you. I am getting a little worried about you. Just checking up on you, that's all."

"I've got a good buzz on. What time is it? We have to clear everyone out soon and get ready for the late afternoon crowd."

"Don't change the subject. We have plenty of time to go home and change, chill out and get back."

"I'm thinking that it is something like male menopause. I feel like life is changing, I'm changing, getting serious. It is hard to put into words, bourbon or not. Look, we've got some guests to take care of. Mark and Bill are good people. The conversation is getting a little deep, but nothing your genius of a husband can't keep up with. See sarcasm—I am feeling good, just like myself."

"I'm glad you like them. Okay, white flag for now. We'll talk when it is just us. I don't like seeing you down. I want my happy go lucky dumb ass for a husband back."

"I'm not going anywhere—call it a business trip if you like. Gone briefly but coming right back home to you." He pulled her close, grabbed her ass with both hands and pulled her up into him. He gave a great kiss— "See—back and better than ever!" He then strutted with his head held high ala Mick Jaggar, through the doors and back into the somber crowd with low lighting, changing his mood once again. It seemed so simple to change moods. It could be the lighting, it could be the rain, or it could be a song on the radio. But right now he wasn't the focus. It wasn't about him. He had guests in his restaurant and he had to be the host. It was acting. It was a stage in a theater. No matter what, put that smile on and entertain. Keep the audience happy. Keep the food and drink going. When everyone is gone, then he would have time to crash. Literally or figuratively he wondered? It wouldn't take long.

He was surrounded by people, yet the fog that occasionally filled his mind began to take form and block everyone else out. It was black and white time again. It was time for the crevices in his mind to be filled by his imagination. His uncontrollable imagination. He didn't understand what was happening or why. He was happy. He loved his wife and he loved his new life. The life of the working retired. The life of drinking on the beach, whatever beach it may be and whatever part of the globe. He controlled that type of travel. He punched in dates and destination on to the travel sites on the Internet and in no time, they had tickets and an itinerary. What happened to his mind during these times he had neither control nor explanation. The destination was ambiguous and random. He could neither explain to himself nor to Katie. Words did not do justice to the pictures flitting through his conscious and unconscious mind. They were like comic book images that took on a real life presence.

He longed to take a walk on the beach. He didn't know how to get there. It was if he was frozen in time. It was if he was frozen in the space that he stood. He heard voices, but they meant nothing. For all he knew it was foreign. He thought he knew better; that in reality he was listening to English and the people around him were those he knew. The problem was twofold; he didn't care and he couldn't do anything about it if he did. He wanted the sand and the surf. He tried pushing everything else out of his mind—the dark voices, the dark images and the darkness itself. He wished for the sound of the pounding surf, the seagull's overhead looking for the open bag of potato chips that some child invariably left open on the blanket. He couldn't find it. He didn't know if his eyes were open or shut, he knew that it was dark.

He didn't hear the sound of the ambulance either as it pulled up to the front of Katie's Place. He didn't notice that he was being wheeled out in a gurney either with the shocked and scared faces of those he knew and faces he just met a short few hours ago. Nobody knew what to make of it. Did he have a seizure? Did he have a breakdown? He was talking and laughing with Bill and Mark. There was nothing to notice. He had a few bourbons but so did Mark and Bill.

Katie was beside herself. Billie assured her that she would take care of things at the restaurant. There wasn't much to do—the clean up crew would be in shortly and they would be instructed to close up the restaurant for the evening. Katie would figure out what do for the following day. She was ushered into the back of the ambulance, she didn't remember by who but she remembered the blank stares as the back doors were closed and the ambulance pulled away.

The EMT asked her what happened? What was going on when Ryan froze? "We were just talking and then his face changed. He got a faraway look and started rambling on about seagulls and potato chips and looking for the light. He made no sense. I don't know what the hell he was talking about. He was just rambling on." She began to cry and took Ryan's hand. This was not supposed to happen. There was too much to see and too much to do. They had their whole future mapped out. It was as equally planned, as it was spontaneous.

There was no stopping it now. The nightmare began. Black circles move across his peripheral vision. They could not be seen by just anyone. There was a genetic coding that unmasked the vision for the unfortunate few. He was one of them. The chosen few. The group of seven who saw things that others could not. Saw things that no others could even fathom. Grey streaks crisscrossed the sky creating random images. These images were messages from a distant being, corporeal to be sure, but faceless and graceless. What seemed to be metal sheets protruded out of the top of the alien bodies. Three forward sheets dividing the face into three focused areas. In each slice of the face stood an infrared camera along with an opening for a missile. The outer missile slots fired close range detonators while the center slice fired long distance missiles that caused a great deal of destruction. On the back of the head stood an array of antenna that helped navigate the landscape, the oceans and rivers and the skies.

Screams of the countless victims infiltrated his ears, begging and pleading for help and salvation from the carnage and destruction around them. There were flames everywhere as vehicles and buildings exploded around them. Bricks and mortar, the strength of a city turned to grey dust filling their noses and mouths with a chalky residue that would surely suffocate them. Gas lines that fed the hundreds of thousands of homes exploded leaving fissures in the landscape. Debris from the ground fell from the sky as gravity brought down death on to the heads of those that survived the initial explosion.

Airliners were brought down by missiles shot from the three miniature silos on the alien heads. Wiry tentacles filled the remaining body mass. Electrical conduits disrupted normal life at the single touch of these flying octopuses. There was no better description than this. They would hover and then fly off quickly leaving nothing more than an electrical vapor trail. Hours after they would depart, lightning storms would remain in the atmosphere.

Blood flowed through the streets as if a Midwest panhandle town's riverbanks overflowed. The stench of death permeated the senses. The grey streaks in the sky were all that the *normal population* could see. The explosions and death could not be seen, heard or predicted. There senses could not help them and the death and despair became in a sense, senseless.

There were seven of us who could see where the carnage came from. It was our responsibility to destroy the alien beings or face the unimaginable horror of having the human species wiped out on a global level. I wasn't sure even cockroaches would survive to continue their existence.

The screams became greater. There was literally a flood of tears in the streets that mixed with the blood. The color began to fade somewhat as the two liquids blended together. I then realized that I was one of the people screaming. I heard my voice louder than any other. It was blood curdling. It was then that I felt a pin prick in my vein. Was this my end? Would I leave my six saviors behind to fight? The vision began to fade, the screaming lessening. The grey steel octopuses began to disappear.

The grey of my dream began to turn towards the grey of dawn. The clouds were filled with moisture, but the rain was being held off for a time. I was on my back but not moving. I felt like I was on sand. I was comfortable but not very. It made sense but it didn't. Sometimes your body would make a comfortable nest for itself in the sand, filling in every crevice and other times, mounds of sand would leave you restless, looking for a better fit. The grey dawn was disappearing too. The voices had stopped, the screaming had stopped but the darkness was still there. It overtook my senses and thoughts, but it was different. It was restful somewhat rather than harrowing and restless. Soon there was nothing. Emptiness. Not despair, but quiet. Peaceful. Restful. Calm. The calm before a storm? I didn't think so. Who was I talking to? It seemed to be myself. I think that was okay. I wasn't anxious. I was floating. It was a raft. It was a raft on the ocean. The ocean was rocking me to a gentle and peaceful sleep. Or was it the end? Soon I didn't think.

Soon I heard the sound of machinery around me. There was the pinprick again. Then there was nothing.

PART III

Fragile lives, ominous overtures
Fragile faith, yet signs of purpose
Choices, pathways, beginnings and endings
Justice beckons towards a lifetime of harmony

XX

It was several months later when Ryan began to pick up the pieces of his life. The remnants of his stroke were still prominent when he first walked back into Katie's Place. He had spent months rehabilitating alternating his time with a physical therapist and a speech therapist. Both were strenuous activities but he felt the need to push on to return to his normal life. Katie had been by his side throughout but he hated feeling like a burden to her. She resented the insinuation and smacked him each time playfully.

Well wishes were aplenty and he blushed each time he felt that he was in the spotlight. It didn't deter anyone from helping anyway. During his convalescence, he realized how fragile life is and how close he came to relinquishing his right to be a part of civilization. Had he listened to his body all those times he had the dreams and put two and two together, he might have prevented the stroke and the subsequent brain surgery. But who puts two and two together and comes up with four?

Ryan and Katie spent much more time at the beach, hiring a full time chef as well as hostess at the restaurant. Dreams of horror were replaced with dreams of the future and a true compass north. They would develop a plan for their retirement. They didn't need to work the restaurant to maintain their "playing field." Their pensions and retirement savings were more than ample to maintain their lifestyle. It was now time to travel. It was time to bring those daydreaming visions of Italy to life. Or maybe out west to Arizona or New Mexico. What about Big Sky Country or even

California? It was important to have the right destination, the right reason and purpose for one location over another. Most of his friends tended to disagree, but in the back of their minds there would be hesitation and doubt. There would be reflection in their own lives. The what ifs would begin for them, too.

Each of their friends in turn began to reassess their lives and occupations. Some would retire early, while others would find their true passion and take it up with as much energy as they had when they began their working lives decades earlier. Ryan thought of the music and lyrics of Sting—the song Fragile becoming his mantra.

One friend, a retired school principal, had begun writing his memoirs, mostly anecdotal pieces both entertaining and unbelievable at the same time. Every now and then Richard Weinstein would email updated pieces because he felt most people really don't get it when it comes to teaching and schools. They think that teachers have it easy because they have summers off. They don't realize that most people wouldn't be teaching after five of six years if they worked twelve months because they would be burned out. A few weeks after the surgery, Ryan was home and Richard thought it was time to send him his latest installment. Ryan adjusted the music on his laptop when he saw the email from his friend Rich. He started with B.B. King but that didn't feel right, nor did the Brecker Brothers. After other selections he finally settled on a live Steely Dan CD. After a song or two he switched over to Joe Sample. He was ready for the memoirs. He sat back with a cup of coffee and began to read.

"THE SNEAKER WON'T STOP TALKING"

Walk into any teachers' lounge in any school and you will inevitably hear the war stories. Some of the stories are frighteningly appalling and deal with the horrors that many of our students encounter. Some stories are about the lengths that educators will go to in order to ensure the success of their students or, that one particular student. There are the stories that make teachers sound as if they are heroes, and more often than not, they are heroes to many children. Stories of students, parents and staff members almost become folklore when they are passed down to the next generation of teachers in a building. Every time you think you have heard it or have seen it all, the next incident gets brought to life. I have always maintained that after each new incident I would write a book, because people in the *real world* would never believe the tales. But of course I end up going back to my office and continue working on one of the more pressing items on the desk. But this time, it just had to be written down. I finally came face to face with an episode in the day that struck me as the right time to begin my educational memoirs. This brief vignette is one of the comical anecdotes where you typically say to yourself and to those around you, "I have seen it all." The reality is of course that no, you haven't because there is always tomorrow.

A fifth grade teacher walked into the office with the sneaker of one of our kindergarten students. She walked in with a puzzled look and handed me a sneaker. The sneaker was roaring as if it were Godzilla. It wouldn't stop with its incessant noise. I squeezed it, prodded it, and banged it against a file cabinet to no avail. A hammer didn't work either. Being the mature principal that I am, I felt that there was nothing else to be done except enjoy the moment. I brought out my trusty bullhorn that I had brought with me from my life as an assistant principal in the New York City School system and began to parade around the hall with the sneaker pressed against the microphone. Needless to say, the reactions varied. But, that's what I do and who I am.

It is of course the way I believe in keeping the spirit high in the building. Making fun of ourselves and not quite taking ourselves so seriously, except of course when we are working with and discussing the academic, social and emotional lives of our students, helps to maintain or develop a happy building. So five minutes in a typical ten to twelve-hour day is an endeavor to keep myself on an even keel. It is this spontaneity and lack of maturity that makes my job enjoyable. It inevitably gets boiled down to the phrase, "Out of the mouth of babes."

* * *

This morning one of our second grade students arrived late. He is an adorable little boy whose mother owns a hair salon. His excuse for being late; my mom couldn't get my hair right.

* * *

The first story that was passed down to me occurred when I was a rookie teacher in Brooklyn. Two twin students were named Male and Female, but with a Spanish accent because the mom never gave names to the nurse, so the nurse took it upon herself to place these on the birth certificate. Then of course there was the child whose name was Istired because all that the mother could respond to when the nurse pressed for the name of her newborn baby was, "I's tired!" I don't know if these two are actually true, but they were handed down from one generation of teachers to the next. So it makes them lore.

* * *

Lesson learned today boys and girls; always play a video that has a real label from a store, not a video that mom and dad copied from television at home. Reason; you never know what was copied. Back in Brooklyn on the days that students needed to stay in for lunch due to the weather, we would sit the kids in the auditorium and we would show them videos. Nothing out of the ordinary, cartoons that the kids brought in or the teachers brought in. Disney movies that the children would watch over a period of days were generally well received. On one particular winter day, I walked past the auditorium filled with several hundred children and all of a sudden there is a rising wave of noise. You could probably qualify it and quantify it in the range of a tsunami.

Right in the middle of the cartoon that was taped at home, comes live and in color, mom and boyfriend up on the big screen. Mom and boyfriend were playing the home version of the "hokey pokey."

Lesson learned—buy videos from the store!!

* * *

We have had a family here at school for several years whose social and emotional stability is less than promising. The mom would often call me at the office because her middle son wouldn't come out from under the bed to get ready for school. She honestly expected me to drive to the house and get him out from under the bed. As honored as I was at being asked, I drew the line at carrying her son out of the minivan in the parking lot.

* * *

One morning in late May, I was sitting in the office toying with next year's schedule. One of my teachers walks in looking a little green around the gills. That cliché will be funnier later, I hope. Anyway, she looks at me and says, "I have a little emergency involving one of my boys." This is a teacher who doesn't panic, doesn't over react or unnecessarily blow things out of proportion, so needless to say I listened intently. Apparently the child brought in a frog in a box and the frog was clearly stronger than the shoebox. She is afraid of frogs. So the kids and I went searching throughout the room looking for Jumpy. I'll let you know if we find it.

* * *

It is just a few minutes later and my school psychologist walked in and asked if I could take care of the bug that is sitting trapped in the plastic cup of a jail she created for it. After clearing away the barely two centimeter bug, my school psychologist proceeded to tell me about the monstrous, hairy spider that she saw in her bathroom last night. (At what point do mental health care people seek out their own kind for treatment?) Since I believe that perception is reality I would have to believe that the spider was actually as big as her hand. I would have to believe that after spraying foaming bathroom cleaner on it, it made tracks through the living room as a horseshoe crab would on the sand after leaving its brackish environment. Through her animation and tone, I firmly believed in the reality of her screaming and the perception by her neighbors that she was an experiment on an X File episode.

* * *

Children come to school with varying strengths and abilities as well as disabilities and deficiencies. Therefore it is imperative that as much as we can and as best as we can, we treat students and work with students on an individual basis. One of our special education students was cognitively challenged. He had an IQ in the low 60's and there have been a few things that he has said that were inappropriate. But we know who is saying it and treat his statements differently than other students, regular education or special education not withstanding. On this particular Friday afternoon at lunch he was noticing one of our school aides. One of his deficiencies is lack of boundaries in the social context. So it was no surprise when he walked over to her, smiled in his pleasant way and asked, "Can I see your tits?"

* * *

School isn't always as amusing as some of these vignettes. On the same Friday, one of our parents dropped off his two children at school because they had stayed with him last night rather than at their mother's house. He stopped in to see me to discuss what has been happening with his wife, including the incident the night before, which involved the police. We talked again about his wife abusing pain medication and drinking and that he was seeking custody of the children. Child protective services had already been involved. While we were talking, his wife called the school to say that she was picking up the children at eleven o'clock for a doctor's appointment. Neither the dad nor the kids knew anything about an appointment and he feared that she was coming to take the children. Now I have an anxious father who wants to take the children now in order to protect them. Three choices face me. Let the dad take the kids. Let the mom take the kids. Let the dad wait a little over an hour until the mom comes up to decide. I didn't care for option number three. The thought of these two parents fighting it out in my office over their children and the possibility that I would have to involve the police was looking less likely as a choice. I was concerned about choice two because of the previous conversations that I had had with dad. I chose to let the dad take the kids and I would call mom to explain.

Mom and I had a talk, which went better than I had anticipated. I invited her to come to school early the next week so she can give me her side of the events of the past. I also suggested that she call her husband to discuss this because it put the school in a very awkward and difficult position. Mom understood and agreed to a Tuesday meeting. Our social worker followed up with an hour-long conversation in the afternoon. She and I discussed the events of the day and said that we would talk again after I had met with mom.

This morning mom passed away from an apparent overdose. It is Saturday, May 22, 2004. All aspects of school are learning experiences, some sobering, some not.

* * *

One Friday afternoon I was walking through the hallway when I heard a teacher say to a student, "What do you mean it just popped out of your mouth?" As I came upon the teacher and her first grader, they were on the floor looking for his tooth. I called for reinforcements. The custodians were on their way with flashlights.

* * *

Monday mornings always brings with it the excitement of the unknown. What issues will be brought to bear, what child will need assistance, which child will get the proverbial "ah huh" after the synapses' in the brain makes the concept connection in class? Sometimes it just brings up the, *you just can't make this up* phrase. Jay, a fourth grader walked into the office on a Monday morning at about 9:00. He asked to use the phone. I said, "Sure. What do you need?" He replied, "I need to call home to get shoes." I looked at him puzzled so he provided me with the information I needed. "I put on the wrong shoes. I am wearing my mom's." I looked down; I looked at him and said, "It must be Monday."

* * *

There are days that are often filled with such promise, but too often go awry. Today began as a beautiful day filled with warm air and sunshine. Our second graders walked to the local state park for a day of fun and relaxation, as there are only a handful of days that remain in the term. Our fifth graders are in the school yard dancing and having a BBQ thanks to our very generous PTA. Two of my teachers brought me a cheesecake this afternoon with the following inscription on the box; "Thanks for all you do." And just like that the day and mood amongst a small group of us changed as Child Protective Services took two of our students away to be left with strangers in a foster home. To the public of course, it is always that educators have such an easy job. Where were you today?

* * *

Do birds need Prozac? Just a thought because this afternoon on a brisk September day, a couple of birds took off from within the courtyard outside the office windows and flew directly into our windows. They were killed instantly and the first thing that came to my mind was the Monty Python routine when John Cleese wanted to return his parrot, which was dead but the store's proprietor claimed that he was merely sleeping.

* * *

Sometimes parents act in a way that is in direct contrast to the argument that they would like to make. Case in point: a parent is angry over an alleged incident that took place a few days earlier on the playground during recess. Rather than come up and speak to me regarding a bullying incident, the parents themselves became the bullies they feared for their child. The father of a very nice young man was inches from my face pointing and demanding that he speak with me now. He was not concerned that I was standing with children as they walked to their bus during dismissal, nor did it concern him that his wife had already referred to the African—American children on the bus behind her as slobs. It wasn't a concern when she told the parent of a certain black child that she should "cage her animal." They just couldn't figure out why I refused to talk to them right then and there. When they waited for me in the main office, again they just couldn't quite come to terms that I would not talk to them in the abrasive, disrespectful, racist and obnoxious tone that they took. I told them I would be happy to talk to them tomorrow. The calmer and more relaxed I became the more infuriated they became to the point that the father wanted to take the conversation "outside". Needless to say, the police needed to have the bullies leave the premises. Great role models for their two young sons who were standing there.

* * *

MY GOD, HE'S NAKED!! One of our third grade students, a student already on our ongoing watch list, brought in a picture of his father—NAKED. After the initial reaction from staffers, they looked at me and wanted to be a fly on the wall when I made the phone call. I started with, "Good morning, Mr. x, your son brought in a picture of you today, which was quite revealing. It showed a side of you we haven't seen before." Some days are just better than others.

* * *

Then there are days that aren't better than others. Today, just a few days before the Christmas break, a third grade child who has had difficulties since kindergarten including retention and a couple of suspensions, brought a Swiss Army knife to school. He took it out of his book bag on the bus and put one of the blades up to the neck of a fifth grader. To the credit of the fifth grader, he did not retaliate. Completing a police report for a third grader who hasn't had the best of times wasn't on the job description. It wasn't part of any of the course work I had taken many years ago.

A week later we had the Superintendent's Suspension Hearing on this student. He apologized for the incident but found that it was too little too late. He was expelled from school for the remainder of the school year.

Six months. This is a child who needs to be in school and not at home. His role models are in school, not at home or in the neighborhood. Two of my teachers have been home tutoring him for an hour a day. He is often found on the corner with a bunch of teenagers who themselves should be at home doing homework. Sometimes there hasn't been an adult at home or if there was, he didn't want to come upstairs to be the "adult" in the room. Once or twice, the student was not at home to receive instruction.

In the case of this third grader, the message from the school district gets lost in translation. He will never again be able to find any modicum of success in school nor (I believe) will he ever be able to look at school in the way he had in the past. I am afraid that he will be a child lost to the neighborhood gangs, the Bloods or the Cripps.

* * *

My social worker and I recently attempted a home visit for two brothers whose mom doesn't want us to have any phone numbers. This is also a parent that doesn't supervise her children well. Sometimes they get their ADHD medicine and sometimes they don't because mom leaves early to go to work. They are two really nice kids who are not very nice to others when they are not on their meds. Mom wasn't home when we visited so I left the typed letter that I prepared for her in case she wasn't home. If nothing else, it shows that we care. We even sent a certified letter to the babysitter across the street in the hopes of getting mom's attention. My secretary just brought in a bus report on the child; fighting on the bus on the way to school this morning. What do you think, was he on his meds or not?

* * *

An email I received from a fifth grade teacher on February 8, 2005.

I just wanted to let you know that Annie's mom just received bad news about her cancer. I don't know the actual prognosis but the father told me it was not good. I spoke with Laurie b/c the sister is in her class. The kids don't really know what is going on right now. The parents are on their way to the hospital today.

I will let you know if I hear anything.

Sal

* * *

There is nothing to be said and beyond that, one of my teachers had a miscarriage this week.

A second teacher thought she was having her second miscarriage of the year. The doctors miraculously found a heartbeat. One door opens while another door closes. Sad but true.

* * *

Let's do a little free association. *"That envelope is bad".* What comes to your mind? If you're anything like me, then probably you have the same puzzled look upon your face when it was told the teacher. To the first grader who said that to their teacher it means just that. It contained his report card.

* * *

This past week for some reason was more difficult than the proceeding 21 school weeks this year. It didn't have so much to do with the school as it did with the idea of family, with the idea of doing the right thing for families and how poorly some families function. After another phone call and a certified letter to the babysitter, the mother of the boys that the social worker and I attempted to visit came in to see the nurse. We are trying to get her to have the boys take their medication here in school so that it is ensured that they actually get it. Another mom has called me repeatedly, sent notes to the teacher and has reached out on several occasions to our school psychologist. She has an adorable little kindergartener who has previously had special education services and was declassified. Although well behaved, this little girl is often unfocused in class and at home as well as several months behind her peers. Everyone is trying to do what is best for this little girl, but something is in the way. I haven't gotten my finger on it just yet, but the chemistry between the parent and the teacher isn't quite where I would want it. The question that I have is who is responsible for this? Mom thinks that the teacher has something against her and the teacher thinks that mom is putting too much pressure on everyone involved.

* * *

Another family is causing trouble this week as well. Four children in the school and two others at home; a high school student and a newborn baby. Mom and dad are divorced and dad is supportive of the school and wants to do whatever he can. Mom is angry and belligerent. We have been in contact with this mom more this week than the entire year. After being on the wrong end of a phone conversation with her, I see why dad doesn't live there anymore. As you know, if you are a principal or a teacher or secretary in a school, it is our fault completely that there was nobody at the bus stop or at home to pick up the kindergarten child when there was a half-day for parent—teacher conferences. How many notes do we have to send home before someone actually reads it? We pinned a note on the little girl the next day so that mom would know that a second day of parent conferences was coming up. Mom wasn't there. Mom didn't show up for the report card conference for her daughter. No surprise. She was out who knows where while her second grade son, who was suspended from the bus, not from school, just the bus was hanging around because she wouldn't drive him to school. The teacher in that class was the benefactor of her obstinacy, her laziness and/or her anger.

* * *

Teachers cried this week. After a Committee for Special Education meeting that everyone thought was a slam dunk, the head of the committee decided that a special education placement was not necessary for a second grader who with resource room services is failing everything. Mom expected a placement, as did the teacher and school psychologist. They were all dumbfounded. I found them commiserating in the hallway trying to keep each from falling apart. At this point, I have no other option than to retain this child, a child who lives in a homeless shelter, back in second grade. Her fourth grade brother won't do much better. He is in jeopardy of being held over in the fourth grade.

* * *

Today I played the role of psychologist. There is no longer any available time for our social worker or social worker intern to see students. We have been referring them outside for counseling. One of our fifth grade students is caught in the middle of her parents' divorce. I spent a half hour counseling this child and giving her strategies and suggestions. Building principals don't often have the time to be the instructional leaders when they act in so many roles. I could have used the insurance co-pay for this session. No doubt I will have many more sessions such as this one.

* * *

This afternoon I had my social worker contact CPS (Child Protective Services) on a family who has presented problems here at school. In fact as I look back on my writing, it is the same family that I wrote about three paragraphs ago. One of the boys, the one typically in trouble, came in with a bruise around his eye. His older sister, a fourth grader, tried to convince the social worker intern and school nurse that she had hit him accidentally with a wiffle ball bat. Unfortunately, it wasn't that simple. As it turns out, mom hit her son with a belt. It seems as if she was swinging it under the bed where he was hiding. The social worker intern called home just to see if there was anything we could do to help her out—she has a newborn, is divorced and is in school. *No good deed goes unpunished.* She began her diatribe by going after the system, then calling the system racist and then had a few choice words about me. I can live with all that. She then told the social worker intern that she didn't want him or our regular social worker seeing the kids. She was hurtful enough to tell our social worker that she wishes that she would never have a child. (And so far she can't). So who gets hurt?

* * *

This same parent has filed a complaint against the school district and me with the Office of Civil Rights in Washington. Several of my teachers and I had to waste our time with four young unsmiling people who asked the same questions with monotonous repetition. They read records and reports and asked question after question to see if our Code of Conduct was discriminatory. I made my case very clear—if you misbehave there are consequences for your actions. Because this child is black should it mean that we should ignore poor behavior? I don't think so. Fortunately, I suppose, I suspended more white children than I did black children and equally gave students lunch detention. A code of conduct, a code of morality for society does not exempt one because of what they look like—at least not by me and not by my staff and not in my building and certainly not by the school district.

I probably neglected to mention that we provided book bags, coats and other necessities to this family when they needed us.

* * *

Just days later an uplifting spirit can be brought down by the actions and lives of students. A third grader felt that he needed to kill himself. He was very sad by life in general. He can't come back to school until I see a document from a medical professional stating that he won't cause any harm to himself. Two boys felt the need to punch each other as a way to resolve their conflict. Two others were suspended; a brother and sister. Trouble follows wherever they go. We simply do not have the resources to handle the every day needs of our students. A third grader lost his father to diabetes this past week. Visiting him at the funeral home yesterday was helpful for mom. He was too hysterical to notice that anyone was around him.

* * *

I covered a third grade class at the end of the day today because the teacher was talking with the school psychologist and the parent of the third grader who wanted to kill himself. It was a nice break from the office. I was going over the work the students had done before the teacher needed to step out of the room. It was about sounds. One young lady added *singing birds* to the list. She then went on to say that it *was really for girls* and before I had a chance to say a word she finished with, *and emotional men.* At last a bright spot in an otherwise dreary day.

* * *

After observing a teacher candidate perform a demo lesson in a fifth grade classroom, the students made their feelings known. *"Mrs. G. we will eat him alive."* From another child, *"He'll never be able to control us."*

* * *

Just another day at the office. A child started screaming out that two girls were lesbians because they were talking very closely with one another. Then another incident where one girl was punching another because she wanted to see how long it would take for the other to cry. It doesn't say much about today's society or its youth. Or the adults, for that fact who are raising some of our children. Fortunately, this is the rare exception and not the rule. I have a school filled with great kids and caring and giving parents.

* * *

So the question that I pose is as follows: If you leave your underwear on while mooning someone, is it an eclipse? I am about to find out from two third graders…so it turns out that one of the boys was being chased and his button opened to his shorts. You can gather the rest.

* * *

Back to the "you can't make these things up" section: I had just finished writing behavior reports to three parents regarding their children's behavior. A fourth child in the office looked at me and said, "Don't I get one? I feel left out." He is one of the children that I set aside Wednesday's for thirty minutes to counsel. Full time social workers would be helpful.

* * *

One version of a pre-kindergartener's version of the ABC song: A B C D E F G, H I J K I'm a little pea, Q R S…

* * *

My May 2006 message to parents reads like this:

No other school community should ever have to endure what our school family has endured this year. The amount of illness and tragedy that has befallen our family has been nothing short of staggering.

The school community has been very generous to the many families in need this year. As the head of the family, let me offer my heartfelt gratitude to everyone who has helped touch the lives of their fellow school family members.

The number of children and parents this year with illnesses should serve to offer all a more focused perspective and an insight into what is truly important; health and happiness, friends and family and our future endeavors.

As the educational leader of this institution, the perspective is on education; our successful Annual Science Fair, our reading and writing program, mathematics instruction, state assessments and their preparation and the type of instruction our staff provides. As the school leader and *head of the family*, the perspective encompasses a great deal more; looking at the bigger picture; looking and thinking globally.

So the message is simple and to everyone reading these pages—parents and staff—lets look at what we are doing to and for the children. What is it that will help them to be successful now and in the future? What is it that makes them happy but also teaches responsibility? What is it that we are doing/should be doing to ensure that they understand, model and show respect for themselves and others? What are we all doing to ensure respect and cooperation amongst all adults in and out of the building?

In reflecting upon our year, and looking for perspective, I always question why it is that a few still look to make the insignificant (in the grand scheme of things) seem significant? Illness and death have been with us throughout the year—I can't imagine anything being more important and significant.

In hoping that our children, parents and staff and their respective families remain healthy, it is also important to hold a healthy perspective. I am hopeful that our future together will be healthy, happy and hopeful.

To those who have suffered this year and to those who may in the future, my/our first question will always be, *"How can we help?"*

* * *

Our parent newsletter went out this week. I had agreed to have kids duct tape me to a wall if they had completed all of their reading during the year. (Principals often do things just to get their kids motivated). So in the newsletter there are several pictures of me duct taped to a wall with captions below. The last caption, which I didn't pick up until someone told me was, "The Principal is hung." If your mind is not in the gutter, then you didn't get it.

* * *

Out of the mouth of babes, continued: "Mr. G, look what I found. It's a butterfly". Then another child proudly states, "It's a *raccoon*". It was a cocoon in a tiny cup.

* * *

Sometimes playing child psychologist is a normal part of the day. A fifth grader in a special education class, who has generally been a good child but typically off task without his medicine has become a behavior problem. He wants above all else to be suspended. He has become rude and insubordinate going so far as to damage items in the room. As it turns out, he wants to emulate his older brother who is now in a BOCES program because of his behavior. In fact, he feels as if his brother will get himself left back on purpose just so that the two of them can be in the same class next year.

After he took his medicine, the demeanor that is typical of this young man returned. He was now, in his words, the *peanut butter* to the teacher's *jelly*.

* * *

The framers of our constitution were men of incredible vision and insight into the human condition. On both sides of the aisle, democrats and republicans alike use religion as pressure points in their arguments to better serve their constituents. As an avid reader of history and politics, one of the most profound sentiments was that of Thomas Jefferson's *separation of church and state*.

This past holiday season of 2006 was the first time parents have spoken to me of having a cross or a manger in school. I am a firm believer in the doctrine of church and state—to a point. I have a Christmas tree and ornaments along with a menorah for Hanukkah and a Kenorah for Kwannza. This is simply a means of having staff and children share each other's holiday. Students equally learn about each holiday in a class as well—to expose them to what they might not know or understand. Beyond that, there can be no other talk of religion and beliefs inside of a school or its classrooms.

I had a discussion with a very nice and deeply religious parent who felt that having a menorah without a cross was unfair. We spoke and he did some research for the two of us after I had stated that the menorah for

Hanukkah was a not a religious symbol. To his credit, he read about the history of the holiday and the menorah and realized that I was correct. At all times he was respectful and thoughtful, which is why his two children are growing up to be the respectful and thoughtful children that they are. We understood each other's viewpoints and corresponded in person and by email in that same spirit.

Later on I received a phone call from a grandparent of a child in our school that felt "offended" when she walked into the building because there was a menorah in the showcase. She felt that it was insensitive to have a menorah without equal representation—she wanted a manger. I explained and she understood the law, but was not impressed by it. She was still offended and thought it insensitive. She liked it less when I told her that she obviously missed the kenorah. I simply stated that it would be both offensive and insensitive to have only Christmas decorations and not have representation for Hanukkah, as our laws have been developed and governed under Judeo-Christian standards. Although pleasant, she still could not be swayed. Although pleasant, I had more pressing things to do than to talk to what could only be described as an anti-semetic. She did say that she had a Jewish relative—but then couldn't answer why she was so offended.

The Wake-Up Call

I suppose the body, soul, and the mind can only hold so much before a hole in the dyke appears. Left alone, the hole branches out in small fissures until it can no longer contain the tremendous weight it shoulders.

My staff and I don't necessarily agree with each other on all things school related. I would like to think that most times we do and when we don't we have healthy conversations and dialog. We do share a great deal with each other, personal and otherwise. One thing that I have come to learn is that regardless of disagreements, my staff knows that they can always talk to me because I will always listen. Sometimes I might even have an answer, but most times it is a place where they know they can vent, share something personal because it goes no further, and then get up and go back to work. The same is true with many of our parents. They have shared personal and family problems as well as calamitous health issues because they know I will listen. I have always prided my self in being able to do this for others. Sometimes my role as counselor could be too much to handle.

This was the case this past holiday season. While sitting in my office on a Tuesday morning after listening to two disturbing events, one professional and one tragically personal, I sat down and stared at my desk. I felt a pressure build and then expand exponentially. It was the heart attack that I always feared. The proverbial elephant in the room strides over to my desk and sat on my chest. He then leaned over, crushed my jaw and lay across my head.

Twenty minutes later I walked into my nurse's office. Yes—twenty minutes—men aren't that smart when it comes to matters like this. My nurse takes nonsense from no one—especially me.

Fortunately for me I didn't have a heart attack. I do have angina. My blood pressure, which is always constant at 110 over 70, had a change of heart, if you will, as well as direction. Although I amused the doctors and nurses with my sarcastic wit and charm, they refused to let me go back to work. My beautiful wife knew I must have felt better because I was sarcastic and obnoxious in a rather charming way. But she wouldn't buy into it either. Several prescriptions and an angiogram later I have to learn to deal with stress and maybe not be everyone's counselor. So I took four days off, which was more than I had taken in the last ten years or so combined. I read Dante's Divine Comedy. It was rather appropriate. I believe that this is going to be a challenge more demanding than the job itself.

So I have been back for two weeks. One parent's cancer is back and she is in the hospital again and another parent had an aneurism while driving. After brain surgery, she spent time in a coma and will have a very long road ahead of her in her path to recovery. Two great kids and a loving husband. How does one answer the simple question of, why do bad things happen to good people?

Two wake up calls? There is nothing quite so dramatic as being wheeled out of your office on a gurney into a waiting ambulance. I think that if I had refused any more persistently, the police officer that responded first to the 911 call would have handcuffed me to the gurney.

When they took my EKG at the hospital, the conclusion that they drew was the same one that I had drawn sitting at my desk after taking a few of my nitro tabs—I'm fine.

The problem here seems to be my inability to practice what I preach. I will tell my staff members to go home, to take care of themselves, to relax, to take it easy and get things into perspective. I know these are the right things to say and to do because I believe that they are. So why then when my superintendent calls later that evening to tell me to take off the next day, I balk at the very thought? The answer as my superintendent succinctly put it is—"Rich, you are thickheaded." So now I know. I'll send him a co-pay.

* * *

Three of my fifth grade students were standing in the office when suddenly their mouths opened agape. One of my secretaries walked in and said that one of our kindergarten students just pulled his pants down. So, obviously I need to investigate. The little boy was very upset and I asked him quietly why he pulled his pants down. His response, "My coolie was itchy and I had to scratch." Thank you. "You can go back to class now…but next time, in what room should you scratch?" Remorsefully, "In the bathroom."

* * *

What are you to do when Child Protective Services (CPS) and the police tell you, "I'm not sure what we can do?" We had a fourth grade student who by the middle of the school year had accumulated nearly 70 absences. There are only 181 school days in the year. Our school team believes it is the fault of the mother, not just making excuses for the absences, but also creating excuses, creating illnesses. We have visited the house, made deals with the parent and the child. It would work temporarily and then both the child and the parent would fall back to their typical routine. The older sister has already dropped out of either middle school or high school already. Even the child's doctor couldn't get the parent or the child to understand the severity of the matter. The final solution...she moved the children and herself to Florida. We can only do so much when they are with us. Who else is going to help?

Then there is the parent who has arrived from Haiti with her son. Dad is expected soon, so she tells her son. So her son waits...her son continues to wait...his wait will be eternal. His father has died in Haiti and she has decided not to tell him. So he waits...

One of our cafeteria aides brought in a first grader and a kindergarten student. The first grader bit the kindergartener because his sweatshirt said, HERSHEY. So he took a bite...

From the "are you kidding file"—Parents need to provide proof of residency when they come to the school district. It could be a phone bill, a landlord's avadavat, mortgage bill, etc. So the question is, does anyone take the time to read what they hand in before they hand something in? This particular parent brought in their cable bill. For the month of December, the month that they brought in, there was a bill for $523.69. One adult movie after the other from Playboy or the Hot Network. Unbelievable, isn't it? That was a rhetorical question.

* * *

I finished reading the draft as well as I drained my second cup of coffee. Two weeks after surgery and I was still having problems holding onto my coffee cup. So my friend Richard fancies himself a writer? Ryan sat pensively and wondered if his friend might possibly have a chance of having something like this published. It would have to be marketed really well, though. The publisher has to decide who the target audience will be and whether or not the message would resonate with that group. Would anyone besides educators read it or even care? He reached over to the phone to call his long time friend from high school. After leaving a voicemail, Ryan decided he should get back to writing again, but in his case it would be the menus at Katie's Place.

XXI

After the funeral, Billie returned home to continue her fight against [the politically incorrect term of] the animal. As she had expected, the animal's attorney had him enter a plea of not guilty. So much the better. She had the opportunity to spew a venomous verbal attack against him. She would have the opportunity to have a predator taken out of society and with any luck at all, have a strong and lethal message sent out to others like him. If you touch a child, you will have no place to hide. You will be given no quarter. The consequences will be severe, yet constitutionally appropriate. It was unfortunate she thought, that the Old Testament couldn't be used in cases like these—*an eye for an eye* was so very appealing. She didn't think that the case would take to long to prosecute. It wasn't likely that the animal would take the stand in his own defense. What could he say? "I didn't mean it. I didn't do it. It wasn't me. Are you really going to believe these kids? They probably saw something on T.V. You can't believe kids these days. It ain't the way it was in my day."

The judge bellowed from his mountaintop. "Okay folks, we began trial on Thursday at 9:00 sharp. Ms. Talbotson, the ball is in your court. Be ready with opening statements and your first witness. We will go until noon, take a one-hour break and continue until four. That's the routine. Good?" Billie nodded in agreement although she had no alternative but to do so. "Mr. Anderson. Opening statement as well. And Mr. Anderson?"

"Yes, your honor," he replied. "I've heard about your antics in court.

Just so you know, I won't tolerate any nonsense. No theatrics, no histrionics, etcetera, etcetera. Kapish?" "Kapish, your honor." Anderson smirked to himself. He liked when his reputation preceeded him. This should be interesting he thought.

He wondered how much of his reputation the prosecutor knew of. He walked over and before he even had a syllable out she turned from her desk to face him directly. "Mr. Anderson, no I am not interested in discussing the case with you over coffee downstairs. Nor am I interested in hearing about your vast wealth, your family background, college exploits and no I definitely don't want to take a ride on your beautiful boat under the moonlight. Did I forget anything?" she asked with a smile that could have sliced him in half.

"For the record, it is a yacht, not a boat and, um…I think you covered everything quite nicely. You've done your homework. Good for you."

"Quite good for me—not so good for your client. I hope he likes orange jumpsuits. Not quite the fashion statement that your suit makes, but it works for me. See you on Thursday." And with that she turned to fill her briefcase with files and walked out leaving Randolph Anderson III to ponder his situation. *His situation*—he completely forgot about his client for the moment.

Well, I thought the judge was going to be interesting, but this is going to be better than I thought—just playing hard to get, he thought to himself.

To herself she thought, 'what a fucking asshole.' She didn't know if she was more pissed off that he really came off as a pompous schmuck or that he didn't recognize her from high school. She was going to tear them both apart.

XXII

The last thing Ryan had remembered before waking up after surgery was an image of God. He didn't remember any of the conversation that afternoon after the funeral or the people there. But he remembers a ghostly image; bearded with long white hair, flowing and floating without direction or purpose. He isn't sure where the image comes from or why he thinks about it, but based on conversations with Katie about that afternoon, it makes perfect sense to him. The question became what to do about it? Was he being given a second chance or is his over indulged imagination hard at work? Maybe he had too much time on his hands and it was time to get back to work or do something. Sitting around never helps—it gives the mind time to add to the picture and generally, it is not always for the best.

He didn't give religion much thought other than to say that he generally didn't give religion much thought. And given any opportunity, he would try to talk you out of your beliefs of the invisible entity. But at the moment, he had difficulty letting go of the images before him. God and religion wasn't something that he was able to get his hands around. It was elusive—it was fluid. It changed and as it changed it became easier and more troubling at the same time. It was his indecision or lack of trying to understand that kept his belief or lack there of both at bay and on the periphery.

In times like these, people would tend to state that this was *a sign*. *"It's a sign from God. You need to believe. He is sending you a message. He is giving you a second chance."* And then Ryan would say, "Actually, it was my surgeon who has given me a second chance. If there were such a thing as a God, he or she, or it wouldn't have put me in the hospital in the first place… And don't even begin to tell me that he gave me a stroke to send me a message. He could have sent a Hallmark Card." And thus the conversation ended. It was back to business as usual, physical therapy and occupational therapy for him and back to the restaurant for Katie where she belonged. He felt better now that he finally put it into perspective, even if it was for a fleeting moment. The fact that he still had moments at all made him smile. His speech therapist had told him that smiling was good for the facial muscles and would help him recover his speech better.

So during his recovery time, he would spend hours watching classic comedy movies and television shows that his friends had sent him during his recovery. At the top of the list were Monty Python and the Holy Grail, followed by Spaceballs and Blazing Saddles and History of the World. He would watch Carlin and Robin Williams do their stand up as well as early Bill Cosby. Abbot and Costello movies fit in nicely as well as books written by comedians. He did have to admit, that laughter was indeed the best medicine.

When he wasn't watching or reading, he spent time at the beach fishing. When he was able, he drove his Ford pick up onto the four-wheel drive beach, grabbed his gear, his chair a book and suntan lotion for his face. The temperature didn't matter. He would bundle up in sweats and a heavy jacket when necessary. The quiet and peacefulness helped him to focus and to relax. The bonus would be if he actually caught something on the hook other than seaweed.

XXIII

Billie slid the key into the front door of their East End Tudor style home. She walked in and dropped the keys on the mantle in the mudroom, slipped off her shoes and walked into the living room. She called up the stairs to where Mark was working in his home office on his latest book. "I'm home, honey. Whatcha doing?"

"Writing," he called down. "I need about an hour."

"How was your day, honey?" she asked herself loud enough for Mark to get the hint. When he didn't respond, she added, "Great, thanks. I start trial on Thursday."

"I need an hour, honey."

What do you want to do for dinner, Mark?"

"I need about an hour honey, and then I'll start dinner."

"I'm horny, honey."

"I need fifteen minutes, honey. You can start without me."

"You are fresh. I'm on my way up. By the time I get there you better be off that stupid computer of yours and naked in bed."

"Yes, ma'am. I do as I am commanded."

"Okay, here I come."

"Already?"

"Smartass." He heard her footsteps coming up the stairs. They both made it to the bedroom at the same time and landed on the bed, rolling into each other's arms.

Thirty minutes later, they were showering together, still kissing and nibbling on each other. After drying and getting dressed, Mark began dinner. Billie opened a bottle of wine and poured two glasses. Mark was working on chicken rolled in flour and rosemary. He already had rice going on the stove when he placed the chicken cutlets in the oil and butter and garlic mixture. He loved the sound of the sizzle. He had a few minutes before he needed to turn the chicken and a few more minutes before he added the roasted peppers, artichoke hearts and lemon grass. Just before the end he would add just a touch of white wine.

"So tell me about your day."

Billie filled him in on the court date and the opposing council who she had known in high school.

"Oh yeah? What did he say when he recognized you?"

"He didn't."

"Shit, is he in trouble. Not even the slightest hint of—hey don't I know you?"

"Nada. I am going to tear him up. I already started today."

"Excellent. Maybe I will come and watch."

"Voyeur. Hey that smells great. What do you have going on there?"

"A little bit of this and a little bit of that. You'll like it. Don't peak. Back up." He backed her up into the refrigerator and started nibbling on her ear.

"There's my take charge guy." He backed off to go tend to the chicken and the rice. "Don't move. I'll be right back to your ear." She started to giggle and sipped her wine.

"So how is the book coming?"

"Just about finished a chapter today. I needed about an hour. But I think you knew that when you corrupted my thought processes to tempt me with your wares."

"Don't recall you complaining. There were other sounds, but complaint wasn't one of them."

"Point taken. By the way, what do we know about Ryan?"

"I spoke to Katie this morning. The surgery went very well. It was definitely a stroke. He is going to have a long haul ahead of him. I told her that I was going to drive down this weekend to help her if she needed it. Maybe we can make a weekend out of it. What do you think?"

"If you want to go, I think you should. I'm going to work on the book. I don't think it would be appropriate to make a weekend out of it. Just focus on what she needs. Do they need help with the restaurant or do they have that covered?"

"I don't know. I'll ask tomorrow. You're probably right—you should stay here. You won't have any interruptions while you are working. This will give me some quality time with Katie."

"Dinner is up. Grab me some plates, please."

They sat down to dinner and talked more about his book on the Civil War and she talked more about the case ahead of her and other cases she was working on. It always amazed him how she could work and focus on a number of different cases at once.

"This is great. Pour me some more wine, honey. So what are you going to call this masterpiece?"

"I'm thinking," and he paused for dramatic effect, "Mark is a freaking genius plate number six. I think it has a certain flare to it. What do you think?"

"I'm thinking you are a jerk," pausing for dramatic effect. "But you are my jerk. Come give me a kiss." They reached across the side of the table and kissed. "You still have food in your mouth, you ass!" she cried. He raised his eyebrows and gave a half smile; a smile of playful innocence or maybe it was a guilty playful innocence. Which one was it? She couldn't read his face right, but it really didn't matter.

After dinner she climbed into bed with her stack of files and a yellow legal size pad and begin to draft her opening statement. She had most of it in her head already, thinking about the jurors and their possible emotional responses. This was clearly a case where people had an emotional bias and she was going to tap into it.

She looked through the folders and decided the order in which each witness was going to be called. She laid the folders in order on her bed and jotted down the names on her legal pad. She would use the list to inform the jurors of whom they would see and why. She then color coated the files using various highlighters which she used to designate the importance of the witness. Certain colors delineated emotional content while others were clinical or medical. Emotional witnesses were family and friends of the victims as well as the defendant, a.k.a., The Animal. They each would tell a story. Some would be graphic in nature while others not so. The latter would be in terms of the feelings and attitudes of the various actors called to testify. No doubt this was a grand stage and everyone had their part to play in the upcoming theatrics. The clinical people would be those like her friend Lori, who would testify to the sexual nature of the crime. The psychologists would testify to the mental state of the children at this time and the long term pain and suffering that would be with the children for years to come, if not an entire lifetime. She would use that last part, an entire lifetime. It had emotional potency.

Other psychologists would talk about the nature of the crime and the type of person who commits these atrocities. Would atrocities be too harsh of a word this early in the trial? She thought about it, circled the word on her pad and left a question mark next to it. She thought about the usage of that word and what it was associated with. She thought of the Holocaust and of war crimes. She thought of Bosnia and Serbia. She shook her head and wavered a bit. Might not want to use that word, she thought to herself. Not just yet anyway. She thought of synonyms that might work better in her favor and came up with abomination, horror and outrage. Obscenity and inhumanity rounded out her list. She felt better and continued her draft.

She continued her list, which included the police officers and detectives that were involved. Tinney and Ranson were the detectives that she dealt with the most on this case. They offered a range of experiences that would offer a powerful and parallel testimony to the clinical testimony. She had worked with them many times and found them both to be rather brash and obnoxious. The brash would work with her—she could do without the obnoxious.

The last time she had seen Ranson and Tinney was last year when they were working a murder/-attempted suicide on the south shore. Ranson, always the flirt came upon her when she was packing things away in her small office. The office looked over the parking lot of the large criminal courts area. It was a suitable office for now, but not one she intended in retiring in. She had aspirations of a corner office two floors above her that had a better view. On clear days, one could see the ocean from miles away.

On not so clear days, you could see treetops covering square miles of residential Long Island and the tops of nearby bridges and lighthouses. "Billie," he called from the doorframe, "Are you still saddled with that bookworm of a husband? How about a little adventure? Want a beer?"

"If you consider a beer with an old cop an adventure, well, let me think…I don't know if I could handle all of the excitement. What would we do? Of course, there is a beer at the cop bar, and then there is groping in front of the boys at the bar. Maybe we'll go back to your love palace, get down and dirty. Then you would vomit and pass out. Damn, how can I refuse such a tease?"

"Still playing hard to get, I see. Just trying to brighten up your day, madam prosecutor," Ranson teased back.

"If you want to brighten my day, just make sure your testimony is accurate, cogent and concise. I'm sorry, were those words to big for you?"

"Sarcastic bitch," was his retort.

"That's why we get along so well, Detective Ranson. Thanks for the beer offer, but the bookworm has some real adventures waiting at home for me."

"Why is he going to dress up like a librarian?"

"Actually, I will be doing the dressing up. Ranson, I think you are blushing. Jealous?"

"Always. Anyway go have fun. What are you wearing so I can keep an image in my head?"

"Goodbye, Ranson. Say hello to your wife and kids for me."

"Adios, Billie. See you soon."

Ranson came in wearing a sport jacket, white shirt and tie along with a black pair of pants. His partner, Tinney wore a pair of jeans, a blue colored shirt and sport jacket that was just a little too small and too tight. He wore a pair of white tennis sneakers, which did little to highlight or compliment the outfit. In fact, nothing in his outfit could compliment any other part of the ensemble. Crocket and Tubbs had nothing to worry about in the lore's of fashion history.

"How we doing, your highness," Tinney asked as he walked in before Ranson. "Long time, no see. How's that professor husband of yours?"

"He's doing well. How are you Detective? I haven't seen you in a while. Are we ready for your testimony?"

"We are good to go. Ranson over here," and he paused, "I don't know. You keeping well, counselor? You're looking good."

"Yeah. Everything is copasetic. Hey Ranson. Listen; today we are going to go over your testimony. I am figuring that I am going to call you first thing on Friday morning. I'm going to ask you what you saw at the arrest, what you found after looking though the house. I will remind the jury and the opposing council that you had a search warrant and that everything that was found is within bounds. Everything else will be fairly routine. I want you to tell the jury about the website and the pictures of the kids on the dirtbag's computer. No opinions, no speculation, just the facts. I will tell the story around the facts and give the jury a picture. Any questions, gentleman?"

Ranson spoke first. "You finally came up for air. I'm good to go. The file is complete and the paperwork is done. This is a slam dunk."

"Sorry, last time I heard slam dunk it was a White House thing and nukes," Billie said.

"Anyway, we're good to go. Nothing to worry about. We done?" Tinney didn't like wasting time. It was one thing after the other. If nothing was going on, he wanted to move on to the next thing. No time for slacking off or being lazy. Plenty of time for that when they were off duty.

"Thanks gentleman. I will see you on Friday. Have a good one."

"Thanks, you too," Ranson replied. Tinney acknowledged with a nod of his head.

Tinney reached for a cigar from his inner jacket pocket as he meandered down the hallway. With his free hand he patted his jacket and his pants until he located his lighter. As he lit his Cuban, he looked up briefly enough to see the No Smoking Sign. He smiled and continued to light until a plume of white smoke billowed out of the front of the cigar. He blew out a long puff of smoke and focused it towards the sign. "Choke on it," he said aloud to no one. Putting the lighter away and placing the cigar back in his mouth he continued to walk towards the elevator. "Lets go Ranson," he called back behind him. "She isn't going to go out with you anytime soon. Go home, play with the kids and do your wife."

"Blow me," he yelled back at Tinney.

"Are you that hard up you want a blow job from me? A very sad state of affairs, my friend. A very sad state indeed. We're off the clock. Let's go grab a beer."

"Sounds like a plan."

XXIV

William Talbotson looked left, then right and left again as he crossed the intersection. He was heading to the Southern State Parkway, which would lead him to the Cross Island Parkway cutting across the New York City border in Queens. From there he would hit the Throgs Neck Bridge and then Interstate 95 heading north. In his Chevy Tahoe he had his fishing gear, fresh water poles and ocean poles along with dozens of assorted lures for fishing in both types of water. He brought his fly-fishing pole and waders. He packed shorts, shirts, long pants, socks, sneakers, boots and sandals along with a couple of baseball hats. He had a jacket, sweatshirts and two rain slickers. He packed laundry detergent and a tent with a complete mess kit and stocked up with plenty of toilet paper. He had packed a few pounds of trail mix and filled a cooler with water and fruit.

He had everything he needed except a destination. He had been living the life of a recluse since Sheila had passed away. He went out when he needed food or general household products, but otherwise, he remained indoors listening to old jazz albums. Not CDs, however. He wanted the 'authentic' sound of the vinyl scratching as the needle slid across the record from song to song, not track to track. He didn't mind much when the needle jumped across a scratch. It was how he and Sheila used to listen to music. It was they would dance in their living room.

Bill Talbotson wasn't completely out of the technology loop. He had his CDs for the truck and he purchased a navigation system. Although he didn't have a destination, it was good to know that he wouldn't get lost going nowhere. The navigation system would help him out as he traveled the small towns of New Hampshire and Maine. He was looking for a cabin somewhere, maybe a couple of somewheres. He wanted to take in the views, breathe the fresh air and listen to the sound of rustling leaves and summer rains. He had the notion that he would find a perfect rock to sit on and just look out over the water, whether it was a lake, a stream or riverbed. Or perhaps the thunderous sound of the crashing waves on the ocean shore. He had an idyllic notion of Thoreau living alone in the woods, getting sustenance from the land around him and in town when necessary. More importantly, he didn't want to have to talk to anyone.

After driving for six hours he found himself in New Hampshire. After hitting route 91 in Massachusetts, he decided to give himself a destination. He plugged in a couple of pieces of information into the navigation system and after hitting route 5 and then route 9 he pulled into the long drive of a campground in Henniker. He pulled up to the lodging office, turned off the truck and let out an audible sigh. He opened the door slowly and lifted himself out. He stretched and looked up into the clear blue sky. He spent a few minutes taking everything in; the sights and the sounds. He especially noticed the smell. It was clean and fresh. It tasted differently than the air of Long Island. He reached back into the truck and grabbed his wallet and walked up the steps to the office. After booking a cabin for a few days he drove over to the site to settle in. The first thing he pulled out was a worn copy of Henry David Thoreau's, Walden. He inserted the key into the front door and gently swung it open, taking everything in, absorbing each detail. He hadn't been anywhere by himself in a lifetime. Sheila was usually by his side. He walked in and sat down on well worn but comfortable side chair. It was a red plaid and the wood was a dark brown which matched all the other pieces of furniture in the cabin. Next to his chair was a side table with a lamp. The lamp too, was made from wood and the lampshade was a soft green. He placed Walden down next to the lamp. He picked his feet up and planted them on the coffee table in front of him. The coffee table had stains and scratches that showed years of use. It wasn't what you would have in your living room or den at home, but it made a comfortable setting in *his* cabin.

He looked around briefly. The kitchen appliances were in need of replacement, from a modernist's point of view, but it fit in perfectly with the other surroundings. His chair faced the outermost point of the cabin which had a screened in Florida room. He picked himself up and walked to the Florida room. It was furnished similarly to the living room with rustic pieces of furniture and matching paintings and prints. He sat down in a rocking chair and took in the view of the lake. Within minutes he was fast asleep dreaming of fish dangling from hooks. In his dream he could smell the trout smoking on his open campfire. He dreamed that Sheila was there with him enjoying it all.

He looked at his watch when he awoke two hours later. "That felt great," he said aloud. After cracking some bones, he walked into the bathroom to relieve himself. The towels were clean but looked as old as some of the décor. He went out to the Tahoe and began removing his belongings. He lined up the fishing poles in size order along one of the paneled walls. The tackle boxes he placed on the coffee table and the clothes he dumped on to the bed.

He brought out the cooler and grabbed a couple of pieces of fruit and two water bottles. He changed from sneakers to boots, grabbed some mosquito spray and closed the door to the cabin. He walked through the brush and headed to the lake. He intended to walk for a couple of hours and clear his head or see what came to his head. Perhaps some answers would come to him while he marveled in the beauty of the area. He would have to figure things out on his own. There was no email here. There would be no conversations with his nephew, Mark. Just Bill and his own thoughts. A sudden terror gripped him. What if nothing came of this? What if there were no answers to be had? What if this was a wild goose chase trying to lash onto something that wasn't there. He suddenly felt as if he were alone in the world. He was on a raft in the middle of the ocean without anyway to communicate with the outside world. He seemed to be living the *Life of Pi*, the novel written by Yann Martel where a teenage boy, Pi, is traveling with his family and zoo animals from Asia to Canada on board a freighter which suddenly sinks, leaving the boy trapped on a raft for months in the middle of the Atlantic with a Bengal tiger. He questions the existence of God and how if such a God exists how can it leave him to fend more himself without his family and with no other company but the ferocious tiger.

Bill had begun meditating a few weeks earlier to try and put his life back on track and to put things in a better perspective. One piece of writing that he liked came to him as he walked along the trail:

Truth in a Walk

Pathways to righteousness
Footprints in the dew
Blue sky. Blue waters
Water flowing over bedrocks in a stream
Finding truth in another's dream
Pathways to goodness
Orange glow, morning sun
Truth in a Walk

Lieu—Shyn

The mediation had helped somewhat. At some point during the day, Bill would give himself up to fifteen minutes of absolute quiet. He would sit in a comfortable chair, keep his eyes almost to the point of closed and have his hands folded in his lap with this thumbs barely touching. He would keep still but alert. At first he would try to dismiss certain thoughts and try to gather others in, but was not successful. He had to allow whatever thoughts in that came and let them leave as quietly as they came. He tried not to dismiss the negative and capture the positive. He just let them happen.

One morning while meditating, he had an image come across his consciousness that seemed to help. He had the vision of a large outdoor broom with thick bristles that was used to move dirt along a sidewalk. The broom was in his head and he swept out visions of all kinds until there was a clean room. Then he laid down a carpet along the concrete floor in his mind. The carpet was plaid. It was red with strips of green and yellow. There were no windows in his room. There was no light to stream in, no visions to see, nothing to look at except the quiet. The walls were bare and of no consequence. The only piece of furniture in the room was a rocking chair where his consciousness would sit at peace. He was at peace for fifteen minutes in his plaid non-descript room with the rocking chair made of cherry wood. For fifteen minutes, nothing came and nothing went. It was quiet.

The goal now was to harness this newfound tranquility and use it when he was conscious the other sixteen and a half hours of the day. The secondary goal was to have peace before going to bed and have quiet and emptiness when rising. A lofty goal. He'd have a better chance at catching Moby Dick while trout fishing.

XXV

"Hey, honey? I had the stupidest dream that I have had in a long time."

"Really," Katie called back. "Hold on a sec, I'm bringing up coffee and the newspapers." Katie climbed the stairs holding the two morning papers under an arm and two cups of coffee in each hand. She handed Ryan a cup and dropped the papers on his lap, walked around the other side of the bed, placed the cup of coffee on her nightstand and slid back into bed. "It's raining out. Good day to chill in bed. So what did we dream about this time? No more of the sci-fi stuff or the killing dreams, I hope?"

"Nothing like that. I had a dream about Al Gore. He was out of his mind."

"People think he is out of his mind in real life, what makes your dream any different?"

"You are such a republican wanna-be. Listen, will you? There was a giant tent in the middle of a park. In the tent people were smoking and barbequing and turning on heaters without needing them. Then Al Gore comes in screaming. He is wearing a trench coat, like the movie where...shit I can't remember his name. It doesn't matter, it's the movie where this guy wearing a beige trench coat opens up a window and shouts out that he is mad as hell and can't take it anymore. What the hell was the name of the movie?"

"Network. That was Ned Beatty."

"Thank you. That would have driven me crazy for the rest of the day."

"So you've got Al Gore dressed up and freaking like Ned Beatty? Maybe we need to visit the doctor again," she joked.

"Yeah, anyway, Al Gore is incensed because the ozone is getting fucked up because everyone is ignoring him."

"Okay, same shit, different day," she interjected. And he promptly ignored her.

"So he is running around the tent, in and out of the tent telling people to stop their smoking and to stop wasting the heat. He's telling people not to barbeque with charcoal but rather they should rub two sticks together or better still eat their meat raw the way the animals do in the wild."

"And this tent is how big?"

"Huge. Probably blocks long but it seems as if it is smaller than that because he can run around it pretty quickly."

"It sounds like a dog running around a table."

"That's exactly what it was like. Inside the tent it is dark so everyone is using these wasteful light bulbs instead of the energy conserving ones. When I try to talk to him it is like talking to a madman. His face is sweating and his eyes are bulging out. He has enormous energy and can't stand still long enough for me to talk to. He just runs from one person to the next yelling at them to save the Earth. The secret service can't stop him either. They are chasing him like the old Keystone Cops movies."

"That's the Democratic party for you," she quipped.

Ryan reached back and grabbed his pillow and in a single move, hit her over the head with it, knocking her back down. She grabbed hers and attempted to swing it but Ryan was too fast and grabbed it from her and hit her with her own weapon.

"So, any dreams about Clinton? Or was your Gore dream foreplay. I know how you like those guys."

That remark cost Katie another swing of the pillow across her head. "By the way, can W spell W or does Cheney have to do it for him?"

"Wow. That was good. Did you think of that one all by yourself or did you get help?"

"No, that one was all mine. Kind of proud of it too."

"Pass one of the papers, please. I think I am done talking to you."

"Sore loser. Here take the one with the comics. It is about as serious as this administration of yours. The reading level is about the same." She gave him a look and he knew better than to continue. "Okay, I'm done now. Truce?"

"Truce. And I'm not a sore loser, I just temporarily ran out of things to say back to you."

"Hmmm."

"Hmmm yourself. Do you need a dictionary for the words on the page?"

"What happened to the truce?"

"I thought of something to say. Now we can have the truce."

"Because you had the last word?"

"Because I had the last word. Now be a good boy and drink your coffee and read your paper before I taunt you a second time."

"Monty Python. Very good. It's a damn good thing that I love you or I would knock you out on this very spot."

"Then I guess it is a good thing indeed."

They read the papers for a few minutes in quiet before Katie broke the silence. "Was he wearing anything under the trench coat?"

"I didn't think to look and I didn't have time to ask. He kept running around in circles like a dog chasing their tail."

"Just thought I'd ask."

"Any other questions before I go back to the sports section?"

"Not at the moment, but I'll let you know the minute I've thought of another."

"I'll be here."

XXVI

Thursday morning came quickly for Assistant District Attorney, Billie Talbotson. She had spent hours in her office with her assistants looking for any inconsistencies in previous witness statements and to make sure that the paperwork for the evidentiary articles introduced for submission was accurate and complete. Her paralegals typed the itinerary for the first two days of testimony, which would include the two detectives, the first responding officers and her friend Lori, who had determined that the two children were in fact sexually abused.

"Jamie," Billie called to one of her paralegals, "How is the opening statement coming that I dictated last night?"

"Done. Its in a file on your desk," responded the young blond paralegal. "Let me know what revisions you want me to make." Jamie had been with the county for two years since graduating from community college. She would in fact make a fine attorney one day when she had the opportunity to return to college. Being a single parent created obstacles that could not be overcome by her at this time. But her goal was to go back to school and then to law school at night when her daughter was old enough and when she found someone to baby sit that she trusted enough.

"Great, thanks. Give me fifteen minutes to review. Please get all the files I need in the briefcase and then I'm out of here."

Thirty minutes later Billie was in front of the courtroom beginning her opening statement. She wore a dark blue suit with a white blouse. Around her neck a simple string of pearls. Black shoes with two-inch heels and a pair of nude panty hose rounded out the ensemble. It was both understated and professional. It commanded respect without saying look at me and what I am wearing. It said, look at me and listen to what I am revealing to you. I am forceful and intelligent and what I have to relay to you is significant and meaningful.

"Ladies and Gentlemen of the jury. Good morning. My name is Billie Talbotson and I am the Assistant District Attorney for the State of New York. This morning I am going to share a harrowing story of two young children...two innocent children who the state will prove beyond the shadow of a doubt, were sexually abused over a period of two years by the defendant sitting across from you. The defendant, ladies and gentleman of the jury, is the grandfather of the two children. These two children, ages eight and six respectively are his grandson and granddaughter.

"Ladies and Gentlemen, I cannot think of a word more suitable for this particular defendant than the word monster. What other word could be used to describe an individual who would perform such atrocities upon any child, let alone his own family. The children are the children of his own daughter, his own flesh and blood. I can only imagine as could you what thoughts and feelings are going through the minds of the parents. Imagine the horror in finding out that your father or your father-in-law is touching your child, your lifeblood in ways that are highly inappropriate to say the least. The words that come to mind are savage and barbarian." Billie paused briefly to see how this last piece played to the jury. Then she continued.

"Animals in the wild protect their own. They protect their young from predators. Why would the parents of these two beautiful young children feel the need to protect their young from this predator, this hellion, this animal who preyed on his own? This defendant, devoid of any human characteristics is on trial today for these crimes. Ladies and gentleman, it is a sad day today. It is a sad day indeed as I stand before you and characterize a member of the human civilization as anything less than human. I hesitate to use the term animal again, because as I have stated and as many of you know from reading and learning and from having pets of your own, animals do not behave in such a way. This is not an instinctive or learned behavior for an animal. Only the human animal is capable of such a barbaric and heinous crime. Only the human animal is culpable. You must after weighing the evidence that will be presented to you over the next several days, find this man culpable of the crime he is being accused of. You must find him guilty of the charges brought forth today.

"To that end, you will hear sworn testimony from the police officers on the scene as well as the detectives involved in the investigation. You will see and hear evidence taken from the defendant's computer. You will find pictures of young children in the nude and performing acts that you and I will find offensive to our senses and to our very core." Billie waited to see the reactions on their faces and the looks sent to the defense table by the jurors.

"You will hear from a series of psychologists who will discuss the impact these crimes have taken on the children and the lifelong counseling that will be needed for them to adjust in society as productive adults. It isn't that the defendant has taken away just their childhood, but in fact has injured them for life and perhaps taken away their chance of a normal adulthood as well. Ladies and gentleman, you will also hear from the psychologist who has spent time with the defendant as well as a nationally renowned psychologist who works with and treats sexual predators." Billie paused again. "Let me clarify what I just said just a moment ago. Sexual predators are treated through counseling, however the rate of recidivism for these crimes is tremendous. It is part of them. It is part of their make up. It is a part of who they are and who they have become. If they have done it once, they will do it again. And then again. And then again. Characteristics of animals do not change from generation to generation. They are gene coded, or hard wired to be who they are. Simply put, a tiger doesn't change its stripes.

"You will hear and see clinical evidence from a forensic pathologist and a hospital clinician who specializes in sexual assault on children. They will offer indisputable proof including DNA samples that proves beyond all doubt that the defendant is indeed guilty of the crime he is accused of.

"Finally, you will hear from the parents of the children's friends who were smart enough and responsible enough to see that children must be protected. If not for the friends and parents of these two young victims who notified Child Protective Services and the Suffolk County Police Department, the defendant would be still marking his territory today, preying on his two helpless victims.

"Ladies and gentleman of the jury. There is nothing more serious than our commitment to justice. There is nothing more important than protecting the innocent; protecting those who cannot yet protect themselves. There is nothing more serious than your skills at listening and weighing the evidence over the next few days. There is nothing more serious than your careful deliberations and evaluation of the irrefutable evidence that will be brought forth. Ladies and gentleman, it is your responsibility as members of the human civilization to find the defendant, Samuel Robert Coltieli, guilty of sexual assault in the first degree as well as endangering the welfare of a minor, or in this case...two minors." She held up two fingers to the jury as she said this. "Thank you ladies and gentleman."

She walked back to the prosecutor's table and looked directly at the defendant as she did. She felt a cold chill climb her spine and brief image cross her consciousness. She stopped dead in her tracks for the briefest of seconds before regaining her composure. She continued to walk stepping around the table and found her seat. She looked at the jurors one by one and took in their expressions. Many seemed to be seething. Others were red faced while others had their best poker faces on. They knew they were supposed to be impartial and they wanted their face to show that, but underneath, their anger and hate breathed a life of its own. She had scored a touchdown with her opening. It would now be up to the defense attorney, Anderson to calm them down and draw a different picture for them. She would watch their mannerisms as he spoke and jot down notes on her yellow legal pad when she felt he scored a point that she would need to refute or clarify in a way that regained the advantage.

"Thank you Ms. Talbotson. Mr. Anderson, your opening statements."

"Thank you your honor." Arnold Anderson stood up in his blue pint stripe suit, crisp white shirt with a red and navy blue tie. His cufflinks in silver matched his glasses, his hair, his watch and his white gold bracelet. He buttoned the top button of his jacket and walked over to the jury. Not even the hint of tension could be seen on his face. His weekly facials and messages kept him calm, even tempered and more importantly, he wore the face of a calm and confident attorney.

"Good morning, ladies and gentleman of the jury. I have to give credit where credit is due. Ms. Talbotson is as eloquent as she is beautiful. She is bright and articulate and clearly passionate. I hope that you will find after the next few minutes that I am equal to the task and can be equally as passionate. My drive and passion however will be used to protect the innocent. I certainly have my work cut out for me this morning. I can tell by your faces that you fully have taken in everything that the district attorney has told you. It is a tremendously powerful description of what is wrong with our society today. I was particularly enthralled when she made the distinction between animals and humans and the capacity for protecting ones own. The words spoken came across as seamless and well crafted, as well crafted as a story could be. The problem ladies and gentleman of the jury is just that. It is nothing more than a story that was concocted by two precocious little children. Not the innocent children that you have been led to believe they are, but children who have had a tendency to be descriptive and detail oriented in such away as to have adults believe them.

"You will hear from a host of witnesses that will paint a different picture of the children and how they act inside the home and outside the home, including their elementary school. You will be shown a very different canvas that depicts my client, Samuel Robert Coltieli, not as a monster, but a loving grandfather and parent. A stubborn, hard driven man, a parent who didn't let his children get away with murder as parents do today. A grandparent who was strict and disciplined with his grandchildren, who he watched after school each day as their parents worked long hours at their jobs.

"This is not about Samuel Robert Coltieli the defendant, but in reality, it is about Samuel Robert Coltieli the victim. The victim of two bright yet very manipulating children who want what they want and get what they want in any way they can conceive." Arnold Anderson stopped to let this sink in with the jury. "Many of you look doubtful and dubious. You are asking yourselves is this attorney for real? Does he really expect us to look 180 degrees in a different direction to give doubt to the state's version and credibility to his own? Ladies and gentleman—yes I am. But I understand your internal debate and I respect it. That is why I am going to stop here. In the ideal world of the defense attorney, I would hope that doubt is creeping into your consciousness. You are wondering if there is any validity to what I am saying? Simply put—yes there is. But you are going to have to hear from the witnesses yourself and make up your own minds. Children are very different today than they were just a generation ago. Much different than the greatest generation—the heroes of World War II, of which my client is one. They are savvy in ways that we never were and have access to the world in ways in which we never had. This is the story of prey and predator as the district attorney has stated. That much is fact. What is in doubt however, is who played the part of predator and who played the part of prey in this very different version.

"As the district attorney stated, it is your responsibility to weigh the evidence and the testimony. You must do so, however without prejudice and without emotion. Strictly facts. The only emotion that is required from you is the emotion of doubt, of confusion, for if you do feel such emotion, you must find the defendant not guilty. Keep this in mind, ladies and gentlemen. When in doubt, don't! Thank you." He looked up at the judge and said, "Thank you, your honor."

Arnold Anderson walked away confidently without hesitation and without the hint of emotion. He walked around his client, quietly put his hand on his shoulder, held it for two conspicuous seconds, moved over to his seat, unbuttoned his suit jacket and sat.

Billie and Arnie spent a few minutes looking over their jury to see how their openings registered on the seven women and five men. Billie thought that she had done well, but also felt that Arnie's story might have resonance with some members of the jury. This might not be as easy as she thought. She was still quite confident with her evidence and her investigation. She would have to rewrite her playbook on the fly to counteract each counteraction of the defense. This might be fun after all as an attorney. But as an individual, and as a representative of the people, she wanted this bastard to burn and she would see that nothing got in the way of due justice.

XXVII

The fish weren't biting as Ryan sat along the shore on a sunny afternoon, although the horseflies were. They left small red welts and often escaped before he could swat his palm across his leg or ankle. After finishing his beer, he slowly got out of his chair and began to pack up his gear. He tucked the hook under one of the poles circles that held the fishing line in place. The bait he threw into the ocean and trudged over to his truck with his chair, rod and reel and buckets. He climbed into his Ford, blew out a burst of air from his mouth, turned the truck on, adjusted the air conditioner and set the radio. He pulled out from the spot and bounced along the beach. He had about forty-five minutes before his physical therapy session. He hated the sessions because they were painful but the progress he was making was remarkable. His speech sessions were going well, too. He was starting to be understood the first time rather than having to slow down and repeat himself once or twice, which frustrated him tremendously.

After PT, he headed home for a shower and a change of clothes. He couldn't sit still and relax so he headed where he was comfortable—to Katie's Place. He walked in with a strong constitution and fierce determination that regardless of what Katie said he was going to be cooking tonight. It would be good for his hands, his coordination and his sanity. He was disgusted with being a burden and being looked at and having everyone ask him if he needed anything or needed their help. Tonight, life was going to get back to normal regardless of what anyone said. To quote an old sweatshirt that he was fond of, "Your ridiculously little opinion has been duly noted!" Or as the website says, "Move On."

XXVIII

Billie woke up sweating. She soaked through her T-shirt and underwear and into the bed sheets. Mark slept soundly next to her. She sat up and collected herself before walking to the bathroom. She padded noiselessly down the hallway. She splashed water on her face, back and neck. She grabbed a towel and dried off. She looked over to the toilet and noticed that Mark once again left the seat up. I'm going to fall in there one time and then I am going to sue his ass. She sat down and breathed slowly trying to recapture images of the dream that left her wet and breathless.

She saw herself as a little girl living in her parent's house. There was a man there that she couldn't recognize although she thought she should. In the next instant she was in court trying her current case. She felt flush. She finished her business and turned towards the shower. Billie kept the water on the cool side to wake herself up further from the dream. After toweling off, she walked back down the hall, quietly walked into the bedroom, found a pair of shorts and a tank top and preceeded downstairs to the kitchen to grab a cup of coffee that was brewing on the automatic coffee maker. She walked outside to the front stoop to grab the paper.

She sat in the kitchen looking through the local section of Newsday before reaching across for the New York Times. Billie liked her flavored coffees, so Mark would surprise her each morning with a different flavor. She sat sipping her coffee but made no progress on the newspapers. She cast them aside and thought ahead to today's trial.

She had spent the weekend reviewing her notes. The Thursday

afternoon prior, she had established a past history of pornography and pedophilia when forensic police showed pictures and documents from the defendant's home computer. Both Ranson and Tinney proved to be good witnesses and held strong and unmoved during cross-examination. Today she would have Lori up on the stand to prove a clinical connection in terms of sexual assault. Following that would be the first of three psychologists.

Billie dressed in a black pinstripe suit with white blouse and a red broach on her lapel. As she drove to the courthouse, there was a nagging intrusion in her mind, one that she couldn't place her finger on. She knew it had to do with her dreams from the last night, but was unable to speculate any further than that. She focused on her line of questions and quickly replaced her blurred memory with clear, cogent and sharp questions that would leave no doubt in the mind of the jury. With each question, she would decide if it was something that the defense attorney would object to and if so what would be the likely reaction by the judge. If it went the way of the defense, what would her follow up question or replacement question be? There was no substitute for good planning.

Billie drove without incident to the courthouse. She kept her mind occupied by listening to the local classic rock station. As Zeppelin, Rush, Santana and the Dead moved her commute through traffic, there was no congestion in her mind. She was clear of thought and focused. She felt energized with the usual nervous energy that is useful when standing up in court. She was comfortable here in court, on the stage. She was an actress with a part to play and how she interacted with the audience, the jury of the defendant's witnesses, would help to determine the outcome. During some of her trial preparation, she would set the stage, so to speak. Billie would draw up an outline of her *show*. She would set them up in acts. The prologue was her introduction to the jury outlining what the prosecution hoped to prove. She would use the end of the act, or intermission as a means to summarize what had been discussed thus far. She used this point to backtrack where it was necessary to highlight points for the jury and to refute the defense attorney's claims. It had to be brief or the judge would cut her off at the knees. "Ms. Talbotson, this is not your personal talk show. Call your next witness." Depending upon who the judge was would determine how much she could expect to get away with. This judge would have no part of her monologue. If that were the case, she would interweave it as questions for the witnesses. The judge surely would have to allow that unless objected to by council. And Arnie Anderson was smart enough to see through that.

Today was going to be Scene II of the drama. The plot and the emotional story line had been established and now the factual details need to be finely woven into the fabric of the story. Billie stepped into the courtroom after going through the daily security screening. The mahogany colored wood tables waited expectantly in front of the imposing judge's bench. The rush of cool air met her as the heavy doors closed behind her. The courtroom was empty. She liked to have the room to herself even if it were for a few short minutes. Billie laid out her files on the table. The folders were color coded and sequenced in order of witness testimony. Each folder was carefully arranged and orchestrated so that as she asked questions of her witnesses she had ready access to documents and notations that would support the evidence. The color also displayed emotional content as well as documentation.

The only sound in the courtroom was the sound of air moving quickly out of the central air conditioning unit. Billie liked the early quiet to organize her thoughts and get comfortable. The courtroom had a certain smell to it. The smell of polished wood mixed with the musty smell of an old room. The were water stains on the ceiling that was in need of attention, but with budget constraints as they were, there was no sense of urgency on the part of the county.

The tranquility was broken after a few minutes when the defense attorney strolled in announcing his presence. Shortly after, family members began to walk in and take their seats behind the prosecutor's table. A local court reporter walked over to Arnold Anderson III to ask some questions. Billie ignored the two and went back to looking at her files. Arnold? In high school he was Arnie. Now he is Arnold. Schmuck, she thought to herself.

Billie's first witness and friend entered the courtroom and walked confidently over to Billie's table. "Hey Billie. How are you?" Without looking up at Lori, she responded. "I'm doing well. Just getting organized. Are you ready?" "Good to go."

The defendant was walked in by a sheriff. He sat down at the defense table. His attorney didn't so much as acknowledge him. At that moment the door to the jury room opened and twelve men and women filed into the box and found their seats. Several members of the jury smiled at Billie Talbotson as they sat. Across the room, another door opened. The bailiff spoke loudly and clearly. "All rise. The honorable Judge Goldman presiding."

Judge Goldman was an impressive figure that was past the age of retirement but would rather be at court than be with his wife at home. His silver hair was kept short on the side and any trace of wispy wonton hairs on top were shaved off to maintain an austere appearance. At six feet four inches, he baritone voice was as imposing as his height. "Please be seated. This court is now in session." With a bang of the gavel Judge Allan Goldman, lawyer for twenty-seven years in the District Attorney's office and now on the bench for the last sixteen years, was completely in charge. He was in his element. This was his home and no one dared to take him on in his home. There was respect shown and a guarded reverence as well.

"Good morning ladies and gentleman of the jury. Good morning council. Ladies and gentleman in the gallery, I want to remind you that this is a court of law for which I hold the deepest respect and honor. If anyone has the urge to say something or shout something, I would strongly caution against it. Perhaps you might think of leaving my courtroom. I have little tolerance for outbursts from anyone in my court. With that said, Ms. Talbotson, you may call your first witness."

"Thank you, your honor. The state calls Dr. Lori Veden." After swearing the oath, Lori sat down on a solid wooden chair. "Good morning, Dr. Veden."

"Good morning."

"Dr. Veden, could you tell the court who you work for and what you do there?"

"Certainly. I work at Suffolk County University Hospital where I am an OBGYN and an adolescent counselor."

"Can you tell the court, please, Dr. Veden, how the two roles go together?"

"Yes of course." Lori was well versed and practiced at speaking to juries. She had, quite unfortunately, had all too many opportunities to testify against child molesters and predators. Looking directly at the jurors, Lori explained. "As a gynecologist, I obviously work with women and adolescent girls. I became a counselor to women and adolescents when I needed to treat many of them for rape and molestation. It was very difficult to watch these women suffer through an emotional roller coaster." She paused and looked directly at the defendant. Billie watched the reactions on the juror's faces as Lori quickly looked at the animal. Looking back to the jury, she continued. "I now treat boys and girls who are molested and raped."

"I object your honor. This witness is leading the jury to believe that the alleged crime committed by my client is in fact something that actually took place."

"Overruled. The doctor is explaining what she does as a professional who treats victims of rape and molestation."

"Dr. Veden, please continue," Billie said. "You were telling us about the emotional roller coaster that both boys and girls go through after an attack."

"For a long time, victims of rape and molestation feel as if they are the cause of rape and molestation. They feel that they have had a role in the act, allowing it to happen. Then they go through periods of anger and depression, sometimes at the same time, others one after the other. Each victim is different in that way, but the same in that they all react the same way at some point in time."

"Would you say that this is clinically proven?"

"Yes, I would." I have done several studies and written for medical and psychological journals."

"So we should only take your word for this as a medical clinician?" Billie asked.

"Absolutely not. There are dozens of published journal articles in the United States and Great Britain that have come to the same conclusions."

"Dr. Veden, is there any difference in terms of psychology where children and adults differ?"

"Yes."

"Please tell the court what differences there are between adults who are victims of rape and molestation and children who are victims of rape and molestation?"

"The most major difference and one that has the most profound effect is that adults have formulated opinions about the world around them and can understand what has happened to them in some capacity. Children on the other hand have not had the opportunities to grow and mature and form opinions about the world around them. They have no appreciation or understanding of why things around them happen. Their minds, depending upon the age of course, haven't developed in a way that would help explain why things happen to them or to others. Putting it simply, they haven't had the experiences in life that would help them face adversity and adverse situations."

"It sounds somewhat Freudian."

"Well, on some levels it is. It is actually another psychologist who worked with children, Piaget. He talked about how children go through specific stages at different points in their development."

Billie thought for a moment, looked at the jury and then back again at Lori. "So, would it be safe to characterize the fact that the two children at the time of the alleged molestations would be unable to emotionally and socially handle this type of behavior?"

"Yes it would. The consequences for children are tenfold greater than that of adults who have maturated and have a greater understanding of the workings of the world."

"Your honor, I would like to submit into evidence, report cards of the children over the past several years."

"Ms. Talbotson, what is the purpose of this evidence?"

"Your honor, I am going to establish that over a period of three years, there was a marked change in social and emotional behaviors of the children in school. Also, I am going to establish a baseline showing excellent behavior and then over a period, a deviation from that norm. I would also request that anecdotal records of teachers and school social workers be marked for admission into evidence."

"Let the record state, that the report cards for the two minors will be noted as Exhibit A and the reports from teachers and other staff as Exhibit B."

"Thank you, your honor. Dr. Veder, have you had the opportunity to review the documents just entered as evidence?"

"Yes, I have."

"And what do you make of it?"

"The children's report cards show a marked decline in appropriate behaviors during the time of the molestations. On the first report card, comments for both children state that the children are well behaved and well mannered and if I recall correctly, a pleasure to have in class. Later in the school year and well into the next two years the report cards and teacher comments became negative."

"Can you explain?"

"The same children who were once a pleasure to have in class are now displaying difficulties with their peers. They have become bullies and at the same time they have become withdrawn. They have displayed explosions of anger at teachers and staff members."

"Had the school involved the parents and if so what was their response?"

"The parents were involved throughout. They worked closely with the administration and allowed their children to be seen by the school social worker. The parents were at a loss to explain. They noticed similar changes in their children at home but thought it was just a phase…a natural change in the children as they grew up, something that they would grow out of."

"So throughout this time, the parents knew nothing about how their children were being molested by their grandfather?"

The defendant squirmed in his seat as he was keenly aware how family members were glaring at him from the side and from the rear. "Objection, your honor. The district attorney has already found my client guilty."

"Sustained."

"Let me rephrase. The children's parents had no idea what was allegedly happening to their children. Is that correct?"

"That is correct. The children never disclosed anything to their parents or to anyone at school."

"So how did the information that the defendant, Samuel Robert Coltieli, was allegedly molesting his two grandchildren come to light?"

"Objection your honor. The District Attorney is leading the jury to believe that my client is already guilty and that this is a recap."

"Sustained. Be careful of your wording counselor."

"Yes your honor. Dr. Veden, how did the children's story come to light?"

"One of the children, the daughter, told her best friend. Her friend told her parents and the parents called over to the parents, Mr. & Mrs. Ahlen."

"Thank you, Dr. Veden. Let's move on to another area if you don't mind. I have the your physician's report describing your finding. Your honor, I would move to enter this as Exhibit C."

"So moved."

"Thank you your honor. Dr. Veden, please describe for the court your physical findings upon examination of the children."

"Upon examining the children at the hospital, it was evident that there was a great deal of swelling and irritation on both the boy and the girl. There was evidence of penetration in the boy's anus as well as vaginal penetration on the daughter."

There was an audible gasp from the jury as well as the family members. The glaring began once again by family members as well as by members of the jury. It was only natural. Mrs. Ahlen began to cry, leaning her head against her husband's shoulder.

Like a bolt of lightning, there was a flash that came before Billie Talbotson's eyes. What was on the periphery last night in a dream was more visible in her mind's eye now. She was beginning to shake and beginning to feel perspiration seep into her blouse from her armpits. She was no longer in court. She was no longer surrounded by wood made of mahogany nor was she a professional, an adult. There was no longer the musty smell of an antiquated courtroom or the moldering smell of ceilings moist from years of under funded neglect. There was a new smell. A cologne. There was a new place. It was her uncle's house and she was alone with him. She didn't like it and didn't know what to do about it.

"Excuse me, your honor. I need a brief recess." Before the judge could get a word in or a question out, Billie moved quickly through the aisle and out of the back door of the courtroom. She ran directly to the women's room where she closed herself in a stall. She began to dry heave and hyperventilate. The dry heaves quickly led to vomiting. Soon the room began to spin and before she knew what to do she felt her knees slacken below her and she crumpled to the ground hitting her head on the seat of the toilet.

XXIX

Bill meandered around the lake, stopping every so often to rest and just look at the landscape. It was beautiful. He sat down and pulled a bottle of water from his backpack. He felt like a nap and started to scout the area out for a place to lay down a blanket and close his eyes. The drive was long and he had nothing to occupy himself with except for his thoughts. Even listening to Coltrane and Miles Davis couldn't help him to escape from himself. He collected his things and walked another hundred yards or so and found a sandy area that was clear of any plants or brush. He opened his pack, pulled a blanket and laid it down near the edge of the lake, but far enough should anything happen, he wouldn't get wet.

He took off his coat and rolled it up for a pillow. He carefully brought himself down to the ground, lay back down and rested his head on his coat. He closed his eyes and Bill found himself immediately in a dream. It was a peaceful and restful dream and he was soon fast asleep.

Two hours later, the sounds of breaking twigs and crumpled leaves woke him up. He woke groggy and was at a brief loss as to where he was. He looked up and saw a women walking nearby. "I'm so sorry. Did I wake you? I was just walking and I was in my own little world and I didn't see you."

"No, I'm fine. I probably slept too long here anyway." Bill slowly got up since the women had made no move to leave. He slowly walked over to her and extended his hand. "I'm Bill," he said as a matter of fact.

"Sandy. Nice to meet you. I'm sorry again for waking you, I know how good a good nap can be."

"It's fine. Have you been up here long?" He realized after saying it how stupid and awkward sounding that was. Almost like a pick up line, which after so many years he had no inkling on how to accomplish that, that is if he even wanted to.

"I've been here for two days. My own personal vacation. You?"

Bill looked at his watch. "I got up here a couple of hours ago. I figured I would take a look at the place and see what it was all about."

"It is all about peace and quiet," Sandy answered. "Getting back in touch with reality."

"So what does your unreality look like, if you don't mind me asking?"

"I am an investment banker in New York. This is my reality check. Some fishing, some hiking and no email or computers. Is this your reality check?"

"Something like that. A place to get away and figure some things out." He didn't know this woman and didn't feel comfortable to get into why he was here. It seemed presumptuous and ill fitting. "Well it was nice to meet you. I am going to head back to my cabin and get settled in and figure out what to do about dinner." He didn't like the way that sounded, almost as if he was asking to see what she was doing. All Bill wanted was to be alone. She must have sensed something and told him that there was a market about three miles down the road where he could pick up all kinds of things but he should be going rather soon because it closes early. "These small towns roll up early, you know," she said. "It was nice to meet you too, Bill. Perhaps we will bump into each other again." They shook hands and Sandy walked along the path. Bill reached down and packed away the blanket in his backpack. He took a long gulp out of the water bottle and asked himself what they hell was he doing here anyway?

He ambled back to his cabin. That unmistakable cabin smell hit him as soon as he walked through the door. Musty, long lived in. Comfortable. Mixed in with the dried flowers in vases around the living room, den and bedroom. He walked into the bathroom, turned on the shower, headed to the bedroom for a clean change of clothes before heading out to the local market.

He headed the Tahoe back down the dirt drive before heading west along a small winding two-lane road. Ten minutes later he pulled in to the gravely parking lot. There were three other vehicles there—two Dodge pick-ups and an old Ford Escort. Bill wandered up and down the small aisles aimlessly. He had no idea what he wanted to buy much less figure out what to do for dinner. He settled on a couple of steaks and potatoes. He would grill both. He picked up a bag of charcoal, some milk, bread, peanut butter, eggs, butter and bacon for breakfast. He knew he should pick up a few more items but he was completely uninterested in doing so. He paid in cash, walked back to his truck and headed back to his cabin where he would pour himself a glass of bourbon, put his feet up and read one of the books that he brought.

He wasn't sure what to make of his meeting with Sandy earlier, or if he should make anything of it. He certainly wasn't interested in seeing anybody, or dating anyone. Conversation wouldn't be bad as long as he didn't have to talk about himself or why he was here. Not that it should be a secret, but he was feeling somewhat introverted. He felt comfortable keeping to himself while at the same time feeling somewhat disconcerted being by himself. It was something that he resigned himself to deal with during the next few days, if he could. He knew instinctively that you can't force yourself to think one particular way or feel a certain way. You are who you are and generally life is what it is.

After putting the perishable items away in the refrigerator, he headed to a chair with a lamp sitting next to it on a table. He pulled off his hiking boots, sat down, put his feet up and opened to the first page of W.E.B. Griffin's new Novel, The Hunters. He was particularly fond of this author who told stories of war and espionage. He got through the first 19 pages before drifting off to sleep again.

XXX

Mark came down the stairs to where Lori and Matt were waiting. They were looking at him with anticipation. They looked at him as if to say, well? "She is sleeping. She kept saying *he touched me* over and over."

"She'll sleep for a while. I gave her a tranquilizer."

"So what happened?" Matt asked.

"She was in the middle of questioning me and she got this look of absolute horror over her face. She stopped asking questions and was just frozen. She asked for a recess and then she ran out of the courtroom. When I caught up with her she had clearly passed out in one of the stalls. That's why she has the bump on her head."

"Who is she talking about that touched her? She hasn't said anything else has she?"

"Mark, she didn't make much sense of anything on the car ride home. The judge went into recess and expects me to call him later this afternoon or evening. He took it off tomorrow's docket, so if nothing else she can rest a day or so."

Matt looked over to his wife. "What did you tell the judge?"

"I told him she had bad Mexican last night and was throwing up. Probably food poisoning or something."

"That was quick thinking," her husband offered.

"That's why you married me. Someone has to be the brains in this operation. Anyway, I think that something I said in the testimony sparked something in her memory that she has had repressed her entire life."

"What are you talking about? Repressed? What were you talking about?" Mark inquired. He was visibly shaken and deeply concerned.

"She was asking me about what my examination of the kids produced?"

"And?"

"I think that I said vaginal penetration and then she just…she just froze. It looked like her whole face drained all its blood. I thought that she was going to pass out in the middle of the courtroom."

"Alright", Mark began, I guess she is going to be out for a while. You guys going to hang around or what?"

Matt looked at Lori. "We'll hang with you buddy."

"Great. What are you guys drinking? I know what you want Mr. Ambassador. Lori?"

"I'll have a Corona with Bacardi. The usual. And I guess since you are calling him Mr. Ambassador, you will be drinking Makers Mark."

"Indeed we shall," Matt quipped. "We are of course royalty. I'll call for a pizza and stay as long as you need us."

XXXI

Ryan sat on the beach with Katie thinking up entrees for the evening's menu. The pounding of the surf up and over each other inspired him for a surf and turf where one was embedded into the other. He had it almost all done except for the perfect bottle of wine to accompany it. The fish dinner was a tilapia with a hint of orange juice in a cream sauce with rice and creamed spinach on the side. It would sit on thinly sliced beef that would compliment the sauce and the flavors of the fish.

Ryan put the pad and pencil down and stared long into the ocean. He listened and he looked. This beast will be here long after we are gone. What does the ocean look for? Nothing. It is self-sustaining. It has everything it needs to sustain the millions of creatures in the ocean. Nothing eludes it. Life is elusive to those who look for more. So then the human spirit is always hungry for more, always looking to see more, to get more and to be more than it already is.

"Hey honey. Before I die I want to find you the perfect piece of beach glass. The elusive one. The rare one. The one that nobody else will have. They come in different colors you know."

"I do know that but where did this come from? What is with the elusive one?"

"I've been thinking a lot since the stroke and…"

"Please don't think, honey. You know how dangerous that can be."

"Anyway, I have been thinking about religion since the day I had the stroke in the restaurant and what a farce it is. People looking for something beyond them. There is nothing beyond them. We are who we are and who we choose to be. Sometimes we don't get to choose anything because of how we were raised and in the environment we were raised. Our parents help to shape who we are by the way they treat us and respect us or don't respect us. Then we grow up the same way…sometimes for the better and sometimes not."

"I'm sorry honey. I didn't think you were serious. Are you looking for something else?" Katie suddenly panicked. "Are we okay? Are you looking for someone else?" All color drained from her face.

"No. No. Listen. Eventually, I was going to get there…you are everything I need and everything I want. I was looking out into the ocean and I kind of just figured it out."

"You didn't figure this out when we got married that I was the only thing that you needed?"

"Let's try not to be melodramatic and focus a little here. Let's stay on me for a change. I'm saying that people always think life is greener on the other side until they get to the other side. It is no better because the people there want what you have. This is life as we know it…life as it is. There is nothing better. You make the best of what you have. I think that those who rely on religious institutions to guide them are afraid to make any commitments to themselves or others in terms of doing better. Religion becomes an excuse and maybe a crutch. My life is like this because god wants it to be. What a crock of shit. She died or he died because god or Jesus had a plan for them. Who are these people kidding? They died because they died. Dust to dust, ashes to ashes. They were in the wrong place at the wrong time. Its survival of the fittest…we are all animals that coexist. Some coexist better than others, though.

"When did you become so philosophical? You've never talked like this before. Have you been smoking crack again?" He shook his head and looked at her. "I'm sorry, but this is a different you. Something has changed in you. I've felt it since you woke up after the surgery but I couldn't put my finger on it. A little more serious, a little less sarcastic."

"Maybe. I think what I'm saying is that in terms of religion, there was no greater being that saved me and said, "You know, maybe we'll keep this poor slob around for a little while longer. He has begun to amuse us.""

I wanted to live. I wanted to get better. I want my life back and I was determined to do it. Me, no existential being."

"So tell me how this goes back to…what did you say, elusive things?"

"I was always looking for something that I didn't have and thought I wanted it for no reason except to say I wanted it and I am going to get it. But there are things that you just don't get. Like…what…how can I explain this? That guy Bill that we had at the restaurant after his wife died. He is looking for things. He is looking for reasons why his wife died. He is looking and grasping at straws as to why he is alone and will be for the rest of his life. He is looking to blame. But he is smart and doesn't believe what he is saying. It is a crutch. The elusive thing for him is that things that are elusive are not reachable for him or for anyone else. They don't exist for him. Deep within him he knows that his wife died because she got sick, not because some greater being wanted him to suffer and to think deeply about religion and come to terms with it. That is just bullshit. He knows it and he is afraid to say that he knows it. That is his story."

"Billie told me that he went up to New Hampshire to go camping and spend time fishing. He is going to try to get some perspective."

"Good. He has to think things through for himself. I bet you fifty bucks that going up there is not going to get him an answer."

"But you just said that it was good that he was going."

"Yeah. Good that he is going by himself so that there aren't any distractions. He is going to come to the same realization that I did. There is nothing out there that we should bow down to. Give me something tangible and we'll talk. Otherwise, all we have is ourselves and each other."

"So all we need is us? Just you and me. We can figure out life all on our own?"

"That is exactly what I am saying. I am saying that the dreams that I had laying on the beach about us living in Italy will not be an elusive thing that will never happen. If we want it bad enough for us, we will make it happen."

"And do we want to make it happen?"

"Yes we do. In a few more years, we are going to sell the restaurant, sell the house and the furniture, the cars, the trucks and the motorcycles and we are going to live in Italy."

"You can sell your bike, but I am keeping my rice burner. I don't know if you can get Japanese bikes in Italy. And I am not driving around on one of those little Italian scooter things."

"Fair enough. That's settled. Come; let's take a walk. The one thing I need to find just to say I found it is that one piece of beach glass."

"And if you don't."

"Eventually I will. And if not...that's life. No magic. It is what it is."

XXXII

Three days later Billie had returned to the courtroom that she had loved so much with a fire in a belly that she had never had before. She was more adamant and more determined to finish this case as soon as possible so that she could face down her new demons. The judge was understanding in her need to delay continuing due to her debilitating case of the *stomach flu.*

Due to her connections in the county, Billie Talbotson was able to see a well sought after psychiatrist who discussed the repressed visions that she was now seeing. He had said that it was perfectly normal to repress feelings for years due to a trauma as a young child. He told her that she would be seeing more of these from time to time as the months moved on now that the window had opened. Wanting to know why it just didn't run its course and get it over with, the doctor simply shrugged his shoulders and said, "Billie, the world just doesn't work that way. There will be words that you hear, sights that you see, movies that you will watch or songs from when you were growing up that will trigger these memories and bring them forward." Anticipating her next question, he continued, "Why didn't these things bring them out earlier? They just didn't. This was the first time from what you are telling me that you have really delved into an issue like this. That was the trigger."

He agreed to meet with her twice a week for the first month and then weekly after that and prescribed a tranquilizer if she should need it. "It will help you to sleep if you need it and it will help you get through the tougher days ahead. Again, Billie, it is up to you. If you feel that you need it, take one, if not, not. I would sooner see you take it so that you can balance your day to day life, your job and the memories that are now surfacing."

"What about the trial? You know what I am dealing with there. That is how this all came up in the first place."

"I won't lie to you. It is going to be difficult at best. In the back of your mind you are going to worry about memories surfacing as testimony comes out. Then once they do, how are you going to handle it in court? How are you going to handle it internally so that it doesn't spill out into court? Then you are going to ask yourself how am I going to function day in and day out? These are normal questions that we are going to have to tackle each week. If you know that they are going to happen, it lessens the surprise. But on the other hand, knowing that they will arise is going to make you tense and on edge. So, even more of a reason to take the tranquilizer before court."

Mark was sitting next to her on the couch in the psychiatrist's office. She gripped his hand. The doctor noticed it immediately. "Mark, you are in for a bumpy road. You are going to be doing a great deal of hand holding for a long while. She is going to need a lot of love and support."

"That's really not a problem."

"Mark, there are going to be times when it is going to be a problem. She is going to lash out at people. Usually the ones closest to them get the brunt of it. That is going to be you my friend."

"So, do I take it personally because I am a guy?"

No. But you will get it because you are a guy." Billie gripped Mark's hand tighter but she didn't look directly at him. Tears began to stream down her face. She began to sob. Mark turned her towards him and she rested her face on his chest. He put her arm around her shoulder to reassure her.

"It's going to be okay, honey. Oh, now look what you have done. I just had this shirt pressed and now there are salty tear marks on it." She slapped him playfully on the arm and smiled.

"Any questions, Billie."

Tentatively, she looked up between the doctor and her husband.

"What about sex? I mean what if I don't feel like it? What if I don't like it anymore?"

The doctor, in his mid-forties, sighed and raked his hand through his course brown hair. "Billie that is going to be your call. There will be times when you want it and when you don't—just like before."

Mark interjected. "No, she always wants it. I can't control her sometimes."

Billie blushed and smacked him harder this time on the shoulder. "Idiot."

"Billie, it looks like you picked a winner when you got married. Most people aren't that lucky. You guys will take it slowly and on your timetable, Billie. Husbands or boyfriends always feel rejected or left out during these times. But I get the sense that Mark is one of the understanding ones. You guys should be fine."

"You know honey. I could get one of the those big buxom blond blow up dolls. It will be great for the HOV lane, too." She looked and leaned. He pulled back. "Don't hit me again. I am going to get a complex."

"She gripped his hand and kissed him on the cheek. "I have a great husband, doctor. Clearly, he has demonstrated that he is an idiot. But, as they say, he is my idiot."

The doctor stood indicating that the session was over. Billie, you have my number. I am going to give you my cell number also for those immediate issues." He reached his hand to shake hers, and then Mark's. Billie walked towards the door with Mark behind. The doctor hadn't released his grip from Mark yet and held him for an instant, enough to tell Mark that the doctor wasn't finished with him. He whispered to him, "You are going to need to be very patient and supportive. Take my number, too. You are going to need it."

"Thank you very much, doctor.

Billie arrived in court with little fanfare and tried to keep under the radar. She felt as if everyone was looking at her because they now knew her little secret. No one though, including the judge, knew anything. This knowledge was kept within the little circle of Matt and Lori and the doctor. No one else would ever know. She and Mark would deal with this as they had dealt with everything else. Together.

"Counselor. Good to see you back. Are we ready to continue?"

"Yes, your honor," she said quietly.

With difficulty, Billie finished the testimony with Dr. Lori Veden. She dealt with the words penetration again without incident and moved on to the psychological issues that the children would face. She then moved on to the children's psychologist that had been seeing them over the last few months. The doctor described the types of sessions without revealing anything that would be privileged under the doctor—patient confidentiality laws. He described their emotional status and the changes that they have been going through. They discussed the difficulty that they were having understanding why their grandfather would do such a thing to them.

Billie asked probing questions about the times of the alleged molestation. The defense attorney would object to this line of questioning as hearsay, but the judge would allow it. While being objective and above bias, Judge Goldman didn't have the stomach for child predators. They were the bane of society. In the back of his mind when he saw these men, he imagined that he could order their penis and testicles removed, fried and served to them. Let them pee out of a stump into a bag. Prison was too good for them, although the general prison population would take care of these animals. There was a prison hierarchy and these slugs were on the bottom of it.

Billie had called the children's friend and parents as witnesses. The judge had ordered a closed court, no spectators, no visitors of any kind in order to protect the child. The defense attorney, Arnold Anderson III did an admirable job of cross-examining, but could not alter any facts or opinions. He saw the look on the faces of the jury. He was losing and he knew it. He had one hand to play before he would see the cards folding before him.

Arnold Anderson III leaned close to his client's ears and whispered something that drew a visible reaction. The face of the grandfather of two aged in a matter of seconds. He shook his head vehemently. Arnie put his arm around his shoulder to further his argument. Mr. Coltieri closed his eyes and dropped his head in a sign of surrender.

Arnie stood up, closed the top bottom of his charcoal grey suit jacket and stepped around the table. "Your honor, may we approach the bench?"

"Step up counselors." Billie and Arnie approached the high imposing stand where the judge held court, so to speak. "Your honor, I will be calling the two children tomorrow. I would like to ensure a closed court for the sake of the family and the privacy of the children."

"How very admirable of you, counselor." He paused to let the comment find its mark. "Agreed. Are we done for the day, Ms. Talbotson, Mr. Anderson?"

They both agreed. "Step back. Ladies and gentleman, this court is in recess until tomorrow morning at 9:00. It will be a closed court. Immediate family only." Judge Goldman banged his gavel, stood up and walked out of his court.

Billie walked over to Arnie's table. "Arnie, if you make these kids any more uncomfortable than they already are I am going to come after you like a pit-bull."

"Its just another case. Don't take it personally. This is our job whether we like the client or not."

"Arnie, it is personal. Just mark my words. These kids are the victims, don't put them on the stand and make them look anything but."

"I'll keep that in mind, counselor."

Arnie continued to file his papers in his briefcase as Billie walked over to the family to explain. "If I have to, Mr. & Mrs. Ahlen, I will object every time he opens his mouth to ask a question."

"Thank you, Ms. Talbotson. This is the most painful thing that I have ever endured. Watching my father on trial for d-doing…doing…things to…my k-k-kids." She walked away sobbing.

Her father, Samuel Robert Coltieri walked away in cuffs sobbing. He turned around once to see his daughter and knew what he needed to do.

XXXIII

At Katie's Place, Ryan was popping champagne bottles while Katie poured more rounds into glasses of her cousin and new friends, Billie, Mark, Lori and Matt. Mark stood and tapped a knife to the side of the champagne glass. "To my wife, Billie, for seeing that justice is served." They all held their glasses higher and repeated the word justice.

"So what happened," Ryan asked.

"I suppose that in the real flesh and blood of a man, there was actually something left of his soul. This morning in court, the defense attorney stood and asked for one of the children to take the stand. It was a closed court, just family. The grandfather stood up and he just 'manned up.' He cleared his throat and before his befuddled attorney could say a word he said, 'Your honor I have something to say.'

"Holy shit," Katie cried. "Tell me he admitted it."

"Yeah. He admitted it. He says, 'your honor. I have caused more than enough suffering to my family.' His attorney turns to him and starts yelling at him. 'What are you doing. Sit down, don't talk.' But he ignores him and keeps talking."

"What did the judge do?" Ryan asked.

"He looks over at the grandfather and asks him if he knows what he is doing. The guy says yes. So he says to him, do you realize that you are going to give your attorney an aneurism if you keep talking? 'Yes sir, I do,' is the response. So the judge tells the attorney Anderson to sit down. He tells the grandfather to continue.

"So the grandfather says again, 'I have caused enough stress and turmoil for my family…or what used to be my family. I am ashamed and appalled at what I have done. If nothing else, I can spare my grandchildren the pain of getting on a stand and revisiting the horror I put them through. I love them too much, although I am sure no one here would believe that. Your honor, I am guilty. Spare these kids from having to look at me and tell what happened.'

"Oh, my god," Lori stated. "This is unbelievable. I have never heard of such a thing before."

"Yeah, well we were pretty amazed by it as well. Anyway, he turns to the family and says he is sorry. He tells them that they will never be troubled by him again. He turns back to the judge, 'Please accept my plea and take me out of this room.'

"What goes around comes around," Matt stated.

"True. But now a lot of people need to pick up the pieces and try to go on." Mark took his wife's hand and squeezed it as he said this. He didn't look into her eyes because he knew they would be tearing. So instead, he raised his glass again and toasted. "To my wife. For trying the case of a lifetime." Their glasses raised, they brought them together to sound a harmonic note in a pleasant key. The dissonance was kept at bay for just moment.

PART IV

"It is a matter of faith, and above reason."

John Locke

XXXIV
Three Months Later

Billie had taken a leave of absence for a few weeks to deal with her repressed memories, which were no longer repressed. She had fully realized a life beyond what she recalled through hypnosis. Mark had finished his Civil War book, *Faces of the Civil War* and taught fewer classes during this last semester to help and support his wife. He didn't need to worry about the income as his book had done better than he or anyone else, including the publishing company could have imagined. His book was sitting at number seven on the New York Times best selling list under the non-fiction category. He had even done three book talks on television including the local station, News 12 Long Island and a trip into the city with CBS and one to the History Channel studios.

Billie and her psychiatrist spent many hours working through the 'grieving' process and learning how to not succumb to the visions that would invariably crop up with new and growing triggers. Triggers as simple as seeing an elderly man with a young child would be enough to either send Billie into a rage, a firestorm of pain and humiliation or a depressed state where tears would begin to stream down her face. Mark had been very understanding and had given her space. She knew that he would love to hold her and to make love to her but she wasn't ready yet, and for this she put herself through guilt, which added on to the burden she already felt weighing down on her slender shoulders.

Mark was generous with his time when she needed it. They would go for walks at night sometimes without talking. One afternoon, he came home with a puppy for Billie. It was an animal she had always talked about having but never thought that she would have the time to devote to it. He came home with an animal that almost looked ready for a saddle. It was a fawn colored Great Dane that she immediately named Nixon after the late president. There was something in the dog's jowls that reminded her of the thirty-seventh President of the United States.

Billie was ecstatic. She could hardly contain herself. After hugging and kissing Nixon, she jumped on to the couch where Mark sat smiling. She landed in his lap and she began to kiss and hug him. "I'm a little jealous, I think." She looked him directly in the face and said deadpan, "Don't worry. Nixon doesn't kiss as well as you. Oh, but that tongue!"

He slapped her on her butt and pushed her off his lap. "Go play with your dog before he gets jealous. I think he might be able to take me." They both leaped off the couch and ran for the backyard door with Nixon bounding behind colliding into everything in his path and things that were not on his path. He would need time to grow into his ridiculously large paws. They ran around the yard for a while until they tired out. That is until Mark and Billie tired out. Nixon was ready for more. Panting heavily, Mark looked at Nixon and called for a truce. The response was a lick to the face. Mark looked at Billie and said, "You're definitely right about the tongue. He will make a fine young wife very happy when he grows up."

Mark went back into the house to work on some papers he needed to grade, leaving Billie to play with Nixon. It was the first time in some time that he saw a smile on her face that wasn't put on for the sake of others and for the sake of keeping her secret secreted. For the moment, she truly had peace and happiness. Mark felt good about it. He learned to listen to her anger even though it could not be placed on the person responsible. Her uncle's death had occurred long before he met Billie. Her anger was sometimes misplaced on him, but understood; understood more so after speaking with her therapist.

He walked upstairs to his home office, which was decorated in muted colors and filled with pictures of Billie and him at different stages in their relationship. He sat in front of the desktop and punched in his access code for his college email. His students sent their papers and assignments directly to him by email. In this way he could read and respond to them directly, even discussing certain points and nuances in their writing. He put on Native American flute music on in the background while he worked. It could be jazz or New Age music, but there couldn't be lyrics. Words would interfere and jumble up in his mind what he was trying to concentrate on. The windows in his office were wide open so he listened in on Billie and Nixon who were running around the yard. She was praising him each and every time he relieved himself. All I get are reminders to put the seat down. Oh, the life of a dog.

Downstairs, Billie brought Nixon in and gave him a huge Tupperware bowl filled with water. While he lapped up the water, spilling half of it onto the floor, Billie walked to the foot of the stairs and called up to Mark. "Do we have any food and dog stuff for the President?"

"Everything is in the car, honey." He heard her footsteps coming up the wooden stairs and coming towards his office. She wrapped her arms around his neck and kissed him on the side of his face. She turned him in his swivel chair to face her. "Thank you, Mark. I love the dog. I love you. You have been great these last few months. I know it has been tough for you. This was a great gesture and it has made me happy. Thank you." She kissed him hard on the lips, the first time in a long time. She cradled his face in her hands and he noticed a tear form in her left eye.

"So why the tears?"

"I'm so happy I married you. You always know the right thing to do." She leaned her head into his chest and sighed.

The sound grew closer and louder. They both jumped at the same time. They looked at each other and both said, "Holy shit!" They looked out towards the doorway as this monstrous puppy came bounding down the hallway and flying into the room with his tongue hanging out and jumped into their arms knocking them both to the ground as the chair slipped away underneath them. Mark's only comment was, "I knew I should have gone with the Taco Bell dog."

XXXV

Six Months Later

Dakota leaned his long neck down to pull out some wild flowers from the ground. He happily ate while his rider sat perched upon the saddle. Katie pulled up on the reins and gently kicked her brown thoroughbred in the sides to nudge him forward. Dakota at eight years old with a blond mane enjoyed stopping often to eat grass. I pulled alongside Katie with my six year old black mare, Montana. The move out west was an easy decision for us after selling Katie's Place.

Our daily rides through the brush of Arizona were punctuated by giant cactus plants that stood taller than the largest man. The wildflowers came in purples, yellows, reds and oranges and stood a foot tall. Dakota and Montana didn't concern themselves with color only how much and how often they would be able to eat. Katie and I would sit in the saddle for long periods of time looking at the red clay mountains that surrounded us on the small ranch we named *West of the Atlantic*.

After the morning ride, we would fill the trough with fresh water and hand feed carrots to the horses before closing them in their corral. This morning, we walked holding hands toward the ranch house where I would cook breakfast. The smell of fresh coffee, bacon and eggs filled the house. Katie waited on the deck with the morning papers as I cooked. As we sat eating breakfast, we looked out into the distance. We purposely built the corral just off to the side of the deck, some two hundred feet so that it would always be a part of the scenery.

Our three dogs bounded towards us from their own half-acre corral where they could run wild. They jumped up and down with their tongues out waiting for a turn to lick a face. One dog puts his paws together as a person might and holds our face in place as he licks.

Inside, the house was decorated in the typical southwestern style. Walking through the house one would imagine we were natives of the Old West. Cowboy and Indian pieces of art in the form of statues of copper as well as original works of Native Americans adorn the living room and den. Muted colors and finely accented pieces of southwestern art match the rich brown leather of our couch. There were however, many remnants of their life back east. Mixed in with R.C. Gorman prints and prints of cowboys and cowgirls were prints of the Atlantic Ocean as well as a print of the lighthouse at Montauk Point. Ansel Adams prints were spread out through the house as well giving it a well lived in if not eclectic look and feel.

The furniture was clearly western. Dark brown leather sofa and love seats with beading along the framework gives it that unique southwestern look. Beams run across the ceiling matching the color of the sofa and love seat. Below are area rugs weaved by local Native Americans, filled with color and dignity for the world around them to see. Earth tones were matched by bright reds and greens that bring life to the various rooms in the Arizona ranch house.

Tables, chairs and bedroom furniture are made of heavy wood with deep rich tones. The hum of the central air conditioner helps to breath life into the dry, Arizona air. Outside, tall trees native to the area keep the house cool and provides comfortable shading for Katie and me.

In our garage, which we call the barn, for no other reason than we can, we have a couple of hogs. Two Harley-Davison motorcycles to be exact. The desert, rocks and mountains make a great place to ride up to the Grand Canyon or across state and east into Santa Fe and Albuquerque, New Mexico.

This is our second retirement and I am determined to keep us retired. Determined to keep us stress free and carefree.

After breakfast, Katie and I walked with the dogs along our property. The dogs marked their territory as we walked. If they were that concerned over the property they should be contributing to the mortgage rather than the acidic content of the frontier. For the first time in their lives we were able to let them just run free without worrying about cars and traffic. They bounded through the brush and through the colored flowers that scattered along the landscape. They continued to make the same mistake with cactus, but at some point they would learn. In their personal corral we set them up with fake fire hydrants; you can take the dog out of the city but you can't take the city out of the dogs.

We made our way to our stream where we sat on the rocks and rested our feet in the water. It wasn't the ocean, but it was water and it was the deciding factor in purchasing this property. Most of the stream was filled with rocks, rounded from erosion and covered in shade by trees. Because it was shallow and slow moving, the dogs made the attempt to get wet. They still weren't fans of the water. They still weren't fans of the bathtub either.

Katie and I made plans to head down to Santa Fe to look through the art galleries and try some of the newer restaurants. They made arrangements for the dogs to be boarded for a couple of days and headed east on their Harleys. One of their newly found friends would stop by and feed and water the horses until they returned.

We cruised down the highways from Arizona to New Mexico, through the red rocks of Sedona and the giant cactus to the mountains and ground coverage of New Mexico into Santa Fe. We stopped for fuel, restaurants and one night in a motel.

The following day we rode into Santa Fe like ranchers riding into town on horseback to gather supplies for the family and the animals. Had there been a hitching post, we would pull the reins in front of our bikes and wrap them around the wooden frame. Katie and I parked in front of the Cowgirl Hall of Fame and stepped in for a couple of beers and a couple of steaks. A band was playing country music on the outside deck. The restaurant was filled with photographs of famous cowgirls from decades past. Décor from a bygone era mixed in with plasma flat screen televisions to watch the ballgames gave it considerable balance.

Our lives were in back in balance. I had recovered almost completely from the stroke. There were no physical effects except for some slight slurring in my speech, which I compensated for by trying to speak slowly. I had to do that anyway now that we were out of New York. We made a good deal of money off the sale of the restaurant and of our home. Our new home with the acreage and the horses paled in comparison to the cost of living, the cost of our home and restaurant back in Long Island. We sold the furniture in Long Island and left for Arizona to start an active retired life. We weren't going to work, we were going to play. The only work would be that of wiring fences, feeding horses and brushing them down. Katie planned on a small garden once she figured out what would grow and what wouldn't grow in the Arizona ground and the Arizona climate.

They wouldn't forget their family and friends, though. People who were with them through thick and thin over the many years of their lives together. Soon they would be together once more, even for a short period of time.

XXXVI
Eight Months Later

There was something to be said about the area in New Hampshire that signaled to William Talbotson that maybe it was indeed a time for a change. What was left in Long Island besides high taxes and memories that could not be shaken? They probably weren't meant to be shaken though. But that didn't assuage his feelings any. He sold his house and moved to a small rural area where he decided he would give a shot at raising chickens. Not necessarily commercially, but something more natural. Providing a life and existence for what is typically a food substance. It was naïve and probably a bit impulsive. Sheila would have told him that. She would have also told him that it was time to move on. *We had our beautiful life together. Don't give up on yours.* With a couple of animals he could learn to subsist on his own. He didn't think that he could butcher any animals, so at least he could get some fresh eggs from the chickens and pure milk directly from the cows. He would need help for the chickens.

He bought a ranch house on a small working farm for next to nothing. The farmer who owned the land had been in foreclosure and this sale helped to pay off his creditors and leave a little for himself to sustain himself and his family for the short term. As part of the sale, Bill was able to keep the animals that were already there as well as some tractors, which were clearly in disrepair. It would keep him occupied and focus his mind on the immediate and the future rather than the past, although the past was always around him.

The ranch house was not much bigger than the cabin he had rented on the lake all those months ago, which was the appeal from the beginning. It was warm and lived in with two fireplaces and a wood burning stove. There was what he needed without needing more. There was no television or Internet service and that was quickly remedied. He wanted to be alone, but not isolated from the outside world. He wasn't getting the New York Post here, so he needed ESPN for real sports reporting.

He had learned little from his experience a year ago on the cabin, but enough to know that change was good and that this would be an important step in his personal salvation. His attempts at meditation and Zen Buddhism had failed him miserably. He neither had the patience or true desire to look deeply within. He wanted to exist and be happy and was wondering if the two were mutually exclusive. He was who he was. A hardworking guy who had a great life. He read a great deal and emailed his nephew from time to time to see how they were holding up after the ordeal in court. Mark had told no one but his uncle and he was exceedingly supportive, albeit from a few hundred miles away.

Bill made no further attempts to understand god's reasoning for taking away his wife. There was no reason except that it was her time. It would be his time, soon. To William Talbotson, it was simply a matter of having faith and conceptual understanding. Reasoning had no place in faith. Faith in of itself was the ideal. To be able to hold on to something bigger than oneself. To lean on something bigger than oneself. His nephew told him that when he emailed a brief quote by John Locke, "It is a matter of faith, and above reason."

Bill came to realize that each person had an emotional bank account where deposits and withdrawals were made routinely. For the time leading up to and after his wife's death, he was in the red, in banking terms. It was his chance now to be in the black. He would continue to lead what he figured was a positive life. He was going to go back to nature as the term goes. He would live off of his land and lead a simple and uncomplicated life. What happened would happen and he would look for ways to deposit positively into his emotional bank account.

Bill met with nearby farmers who were more than happy to help the 'city slicker' become comfortable with the business and life of the farmer. Over time he began to spend more time in the small town meeting people of his own age and was surprised to find more similarities than he had thought. He was even more surprised to find how politically involved farmers were in the process and reaching out to their representatives. Equally, how adept they were at convincing their representatives that their continued support would depend upon the representatives continued push for their pork barrel initiatives, without which, neither could survive. Bill was fascinated by their strength and their dogged determination in the face of adversity and economic and political pressure.

He found the grassroots political process of the rural towns refreshing and invigorating. Living in a metropolitan area or suburb of, you didn't have the type of access you did here where the population was significantly smaller. The politician here was your neighbor and unless they were flying to Washington D.C., where they had limousines and navy blue suits, you would find them in their pick up trucks heading to town hall meetings or to town to do what they needed to keep their farm moving forward. The long term politician might parcel off pieces of their property or sell it altogether so that they wouldn't find themselves in bankruptcy or in a position to be called a negligent farmer, leaving their crops to go wild or to whither in the sun.

One evening, Bill met a woman in the local bar and grilles. He had seen her there before but never showed any interest, except to sometimes look too long hoping she would notice. He knew her name from the bartender, but would have inevitably found out anyway as everyone knew each other in town. She would look quickly away and then just as quickly look back over to see if he had looked away. It was flirtatious and cute, but he didn't think he was ready for a relationship, although he was beginning to feel the effects of living alone. Too much solitude could be too sequestration, too quiet and too lonely.

He thought the right thing to do would be to find out what she was drinking and send one over with his compliments. Then he thought better of it. He caught enough courage and simply walked over to the tall, lithe redhead, offered his hand and introduced himself. She responded in kind saying that her name was Terry. She too had lost her spouse but didn't quite know the way to approach a man. It had been a very long time since she had been on a date, let alone talk intimately with another man other than her husband.

Bill and Terry shared some simple things about themselves, where they came from, if they had children and where they were and what they were doing. After a couple of drinks they settled in at a booth and ordered some wine and some dinner. Thus began the second chapter and second chance at life for William Talbotson, formerly of New York, now a farmer in small town New Hampshire. Perhaps this was god's way. One door closes and another door opens, Sheila used to say. "Take a chance and walk through it," he would remember her saying years ago when looking for another job. It was the same thing he had told his nephew when he was first thinking of proposing to Billie.

PART V

Believing in something is more important than believing in nothing. Even if it is a naïve belief; there is an opportunity to hold on to something outside of ourselves.

XXXVII

They gathered together for the first time since the afternoon following the funeral for Sheila Talbotson. That had been nearly two years ago and much had happened in the time between. Lives had been put back together; Ryan and Katie, Bill and Terry, while others were still working on regaining the vitality and vigor of the life they had; Billie and Mark.

Ryan and Katie had done well for themselves and without taking no for an answer, they flew out many of the people who helped shape who they were and had become as well as who helped them realize that change is good, that moving on is good. Revelations are elusive sometimes and it is those who seek to better themselves, spiritually, socially and/or economically, who prosper from the realization of something better, of something that may be beyond them to help them and to guide them forward.

Gifts were not to be brought, although they were. How could someone come empty handed when they were just flown out and picked up from the airport by limousine? So their guests, too would not take no for an answer. There were things for the house, things for the bar, things for Katie, things for Ryan and things for Dakota and Montana. The dogs sat eagerly waiting for something for them. They too would get something new. Happy with their bones, they left for a quiet area to chew and claw undisturbed.

In their living room stood a seven-foot potted cactus tastefully decorated with lights, ornaments and garland. Each of the guests in turn had to take a picture with the *Christmas Cactus*. It was the same picture that Ryan and Katie used for their greeting cards and their invitation to Christmas in Arizona.

Among the guests that included their restaurant friends and their beach friends, were family and their friends. Billie and Mark, Lori and Matt, Bill and his girlfriend Terry and President Nixon. All told there were 16 guests and one Great Dane whose appetite surpassed everyone else's including Montana and Dakota. President Nixon loved to run the ranch and play with Ryan and Katie's three dogs. President Nixon was better suited though to play with the horses.

At the bar, Ryan took out the bottle he had intended to open the night he had had the stroke. Mark, Matt and Bill shook in a circular fashion the nose glass filled with caramel goodness, Old Foresters' Birthday Bourbon. Not expensive, but not easy to get either. While waiting for Ryan's direction, they each placed the nose glass to their nose and inhaled deeply. They each looked at each other and smiled. Matt looked at Mark. Mark knew what he was going to say. "Tonight we drink, tomorrow we fight!"

"Couldn't have said it better myself," Ryan stated. "To friends and family".

"To friends and family," they each replied. And then they drank. And they enjoyed. And it was good. Ryan took out another bottle. "This is the other bourbon I would like you to try this evening my friends. Pappy Van Winkle."

It was Bill who spoke up. "Life is good. Life is good."

"Do tell Uncle Bill, do tell." William Talbotson began to talk about the last two years and what he had discovered and whom he discovered. And when he finished forty-five minutes later, he looked at his newly refilled glass and stated, "Tonight we may drink, but tomorrow is for tomorrow. There is no need to fight. There is only to find yourself and share it with someone else."

"There's nothing better that could be said than that," said Matt.

"So Ryan," began Mark, "Why Arizona?"

"Good question. And speaking of tomorrow, providing of course that your hangovers don't get in the way, and may I suggest two Tylenol before bed, you will see why Arizona. I have rented horses for all of you. You will see why Arizona."

"Merry Christmas too all of us, then," Matt said.

"And speaking of Christmas…Ryan I remember you saying once how hard it was to come by that elusive thing. You spoke about it that afternoon at your restaurant."

"Bill, I would love to tell you that I remember what we spoke about, but I have only fragments. I don't remember most of what was said, although Katie said we actually sounded intelligent. But elusive is a word that I would have definitely used."

Bill reached into his pocket. I know how much you loved the beach, which I can only imagine that you miss, but I remember how much you wanted to get Katie this elusive something."

Ryan became very quiet and tried to rack his mind for what he might have said. His eyebrows raised as if puzzled.

Bill smiled and pulled his hand out of his pocket. "Not everything needs to be elusive, young man. Here is a gift from me to you for your beautiful wife. It belonged to Sheila. And as you have said in your own words, I won't take no for an answer."

Bill reached across to Ryan and opened his hand. Sitting there, sharp as a crystal and as bright as a diamond were the elusive ones. The ones that he and Katie would walk the beach for but never find. Beach glass; one red and one yellow and one purple.

"I don't know what to say, Bill, except thank you. Are you sure you want to part with these"?

"Sheila loved beach glass. Frankly, I never understood it, but I did understand that if it was important to her, it was important to me. If it was that important to you to find it for your wife, Sheila would want it to go to someone who would treasure it as much as she did."

"Is this what you learned in New Hampshire on that fishing trip last year, Uncle Bill?"

"That and this." He paused to gather his thoughts so that what he said would come out just as he wanted it to. "We all have a story. We all tell it to ourselves when nobody is around. It isn't necessarily the story that we tell each other because there are things that we rather not say. Our story is created from our past, from what is given to us, what we inherit and what we see and hear. We each see the same and hear the same but we weave a different story for ourselves, to make it make sense to ourselves. Ryan, that night in your restaurant you said that you never look back, you only look forward." Ryan nodded his head in agreement. "But that isn't necessarily true, with all due respect. Thanks for the invitation and the bourbon. But what I am saying is that your past is your future. You can choose to ignore it or choose to live with it and use it. You Mark, the history professor should know this better than anyone sitting at this table.

"What it comes down to is faith. And when I say faith I am not saying a belief in god, although I could be saying that. It is a faith in yourself. A faith that you will know how to address adversity and pain and come through it with as few scars as possible. If it means that you look within to find the strength and courage and conviction to move past the obstacle and find that balance in your life, then so be it. But for others, myself included, I have to have faith that the world itself will do the right thing for all of us. I believe that there is something looking over us, a god, a spirit, or even the belief that there is something there to reach for when their is no one else to reach for. Believing in something is more important than believing in nothing. What that something is, well that is up to you and what you make of it."

"Are we talking Bible beliefs? Are we talking an existential belief?" Mark asked.

"I am saying that the Bible is part of our story. Our lives are a story that you are the author of. You are in control of it. You determine the outcomes and when chapters end and begin. The Bible is a book of great stories. Men wrote the stories. I don't know if Moses came down with tablets or that God "smite" people and opened up rivers and sent locusts and all of that. The stories are simply a place for people to have their faith placed, if they want.

What I am trying to get at, and maybe it is the fine bourbon, but, having something is better than having nothing at all. What do they say, whatever gets you through the night."

"That or whatever floats your boat. Cheers, Uncle Bill."

"To all of us and to all of our stories. Cheers," Ryan said.

"To all of us. Merry Christmas, if that is what you would like," Matt finished and held up his glass.

They drank up and poured another glass of bourbon.

Afterword

They say that the grass is always greener on the other side. That may be so. But what fertilizer are they using? It isn't likely to be organic which means that the poisons that they are putting on their grass will come back to bite them in the ass. Interpretation: stay where you are and don't worry about what others are doing. Make what you have work!

This story is a work of fiction except where it is not. The characters in this story are a work of fiction except where it may not be. Everything else is true as much as fiction can be true. If you recognize yourself as one of the characters or know someone who resembles one of the characters than you have realized that fiction in some fashion, can be truth. While reading this story, I hope that you have come to the revelation that life is what we make of it and how we persevere through adversity.

(The only true truth in the book was the memoirs of the retired principal, *Richard Weinstein*. I am neither Richard Weinstein nor am I retired. I changed my name to protect the innocent—me! Those vignettes are only half of the things that have actually happened to me as an educator in a twenty-four year career, so far. The other half is for another time. Perhaps).

How many of us have questioned their faith and their beliefs; their core beliefs? We learned these beliefs from our parents who passed it down from their parents. We went to synagogue, we went to church, to a mosque and Buddhist temples. We may pray to many spirits, the spirit

214

of rain, of the sun, of the earth and sky. We believed what we were told to believe until we began to ask questions.

There are many people across the globe that do not question their beliefs, their governments or the newspapers they read. The blindly follow the path that has been handed to them by those whom they think are superior in intellect and in status. But they are neither. Those who do not question are doomed to be insufferable and closed minded as well as being insufferably closed-minded.

Situations change. I'm not so sure about how much people can change. Sometimes it is nice to be surprised. Take a chance. Ask yourself questions. Did God split the river in half so that Moses and his people could cross or was it a scientific phenomenon? Probably a little to coincidental for that. Perhaps the bibles are just great stories handed down by the people who wrote them.

CRIME IN FITNESS

by Richard Wood

The story reveals many of the true crimes in the fitness industry as well as a murder. The main character finds he is in business with someone who has been hiding his true identity. The evolution of the health club industry in the early 70's is displayed when Dubois starts as an instructor for a health club. Making mistakes along the way, he builds a chain of clubs in Texas only to lose them to a mentor. Finding another chance to do it right, he is shocked to find he has ended up in a similar situation. The man with the hidden identity offers Dubois assistance when Dubois finds himself at the scene of a murder. Numerous characters appear to be possibly responsible. The main character is also going through a serious time with his personal life as he and his wife try to have children. They find out that after many tests the only possibility they have is through in vitro fertilization.

Paperback, 150 pages
5.5" x 8.5"
ISBN 1-4137-1399-8

About the author:

Richard Wood got his start in the fitness industry when he went to work as an instructor for New Life Health Spa in Lima, Ohio. Becoming the youngest man to be voted to the position as director on the prestigious board of the Association of Physical Fitness Centers, he was active in the development of legislation regulating that industry. RichardWood333@aol.com

THE LITTLE BOY OF THE FOREST

by J.A. Aarntzen

Jack Thurston eagerly awaited his return to Black Island, his mother's family retreat in Canada's wild and pristine cottage country of 1929. Yet when the young lad of ten arrived, no one would have anything to do with him, not his grandfather, not his aunt and uncle, his cousins, not even his mother. He soon discovered that the physical world itself would not interact with him. He no longer possessed even the simple skill of opening a door. The only ones that took note of him were two eerie strangers, a haggard old woman and a creepy little boy that seemed to be always lurking in the shadows. When his grandfather suddenly took ill, Jack knew that these strangers were somehow connected. The urgency of his grandfather's condition demanded that he be rushed to the hospital at once. The worried and distressed family went along with the dying old man. They somehow had forgotten Jack. He was left by himself trapped inside the cottage on Black Island with nobody other than the two strangers who were trying to get in.

Paperback, 522 pages
6" x 9"
ISBN 1-4137-8055-5

The Little Boy of the Forest follows Jack's odyssey into loneliness and fear with his undying hope that one day his family will return.

About the author:

J.A. Aarntzen has been crafting tales of fantasy and adventure since 1978. *The Little Boy of the Forest* is his first foray into ghost stories and is his first published work. An avid enthusiast of nature, he lives in the Canadian hinterland with his wife, Laura, and his dog Sarah.

also available from publishamerica

DROPS OF DEW
by Ashok Sinha

Drops of Dew is a collection of fifty poems by Ashok Sinha written during the mid-60s and mid-70s. During this period, Ashok Sinha traveled from India to the United States where he was a student and, subsequently, a research fellow (NASA), respectively. The poems mostly reflect emotional response to this transitional phase and related reactions in terms of love, separation, anticipation, etc. with a Sufi-like quality where the object of love is often identified with God. An underlying tone of positivity is usually present in most of the poems. Also, there are poems that deride human fragility or social aberration with a touch of humor. The reader is likely to identify his or her feelings with the themes of these poems most naturally.

Paperback, 79 pages
6" x 9"
ISBN 1-4241-8120-8

About the author:

Ashok Sinha was born in India on January 8, 1943. After completing a master's degree in physics, he traveled to USA to join the University of Maryland, where he worked as a graduate student and, subsequently, as a post-doctoral research fellow. His interests include poetry/literature as well as physics/science. He has several books and publications in both areas, in English and in Hindi (his native language) to his credit.

available to all bookstores nationwide.
www.publishamerica.com

THE FINAL MISSION
GRANT AND LEE

by George Miga

It is 1870, and the nation is still badly splintered by civil war. Ulysses S. Grant, two years into a presidency tainted by scandal, struggles to unite the country. He believes only one man can help him convince the factions to bury the gauntlet—a man admired more in the South and North than the general who won the war—Robert E. Lee. Grant assigns his young security chief, Colonel John Spencer, to persuade a reluctant Lee to invite the President to the first reunion of the senior officers of the Army of Northern Virginia. Grant believes the symbolism of his standing with Lee in front of the elite of the Confederate military will help diminish the bitterness. Colonel Spencer, with the help of General William T. Sherman, the President's trusted friend, learns that KKK assassins will attempt to prevent the meeting by killing Spencer—and the President.

Paperback, 271 pages
6" x 9"
ISBN 1-4241-7987-4

About the author:

George P. Miga, a Crisis Management and Communications Consultant, is an adjunct faculty member of Indiana University Northwest's Graduate School of Business and Economics. As a manager for Amoco Corp., he worked on a project with former Presidents Ford and Nixon. He was a commercial charter pilot and newspaper reporter.